# *PO*

## *a unique woman who touches the world!*

*"Denise Turney's is a new, different and compelling voice. She relates poverty and base reality so that it clutches at you even as snippets of polished sophistication lull you into believing that the rawness of life is ephemeral. The dignity of her characters leaps from the pages, and neither poverty, a frightening illness nor an all-powerful need for love and affection can camouflage it . . ."*

**Gwynne Forster**
**Author of Ecstasy and Obsession**

### PORTIA!

**a powerful, unforgettable woman who knows how to live!
you won't forget PORTIA!**

**by denise turney**

# PORTIA

**Copyright 1997**
Chistell Publishing
First Printing, May 1998
Second Printing, January 2000


Scriptures are taken from the
New International Version of the Bible.
Copyright 1985, Zondervan Corporation

Published by:        Chistell Publishing
                     2500 Knights Road, Suite 19-01
                     Bensalem, PA  19020

Cover:  Morris Publishing

ISBN:  0-9663539-0-0
Library of Congress Catalog Card Number:  97-068440


Printed in the USA by

MORRIS PUBLISHING

3212 East Highway 30 • Kearney, NE 68847 • 1-800-650-7888

# *Dedication*

*for my son, Gregory*

# *Acknowledgments*

This story is dedicated to women, men, children, their friends, family members and loved ones who have had their lives challenged by cancer of any type. Furthermore, this story is dedicated to the physicians, nurses and other medical professionals who have worked to heal our bodies.

I thank my family. My father, Richard Turney, who raised my brothers, sister and I as a single parent after the death of our mother. My father; my hero. My mother, Doris Jean. She showed me what a beautiful woman was -- her -- Mommie. My brothers, Richard, Clark and Eric. They are my friends and men I look up to. My sister, Adrianne. One of my very best friends. My dear sister. My grandparents, Clyde and Emma Turney, Jr. Mountains of strength in our family. Where my root returns to. I admire them and love them beyond the scope of human intellect or expression. My aunts, Patricia and Christine. I love you with all of my heart. My uncle, Donald. A kind and loving man. My cousins, Donna, Monica, Michael and Langston. You are so very special. I love you. My sister-in-laws, Doris and Nina. You are true sisters. My brother-in-law, Ricky Daniels. It is a pleasure having you in our family. To my nieces, Angel and Assyria -- you are the apples of my eye. Cutie pies. To my nephew, Richard. I love you. To my friends and loved ones: Felicia Wells, Linda (Flip), Pam Robinson, Cormy L. Williams, Willie J. Murray, Martha Miller, Carolyn, Joseph, Artie, Essie and Tim Stackhouse, Helen Crawford and each of my Sigma Gamma Rho Sorority, Incorporated sorors. [If I forgot anyone, charge it to my head and not my heart, then put your name (here).] Thanks for all of your love, kindness, prayers, encouragement, spirit and support. To my church family--Norton Avenue First Baptist Church. To my pastor and his lovely wife, Rev. James Evans III and Sheila Evans. Go in God's strength! I love you all! To Nancy Delaney, Billy Ryder, Gwen Shrift, Patricia White, The American Cancer Society, The National Cancer Institute and the members of WRITE. To the woman who designed my web page and who keeps visitors coming, Anna Stevens of ALG Designs. Thank you for your invaluable assistance. To PORTIA's readers. Thank you for believing in PORTIA. I hope you fall in love with her the way I did. Happy reading!

# *Table of Contents*

*Because I want you to know that you are not alone . . .*

**Information about breast cancer and cancer in general can be found at:**

The American Cancer Society
1-800-227-2345
http://www.cancer.org/frames.html

National Institute for Cancer
1-800-422-6237

OncoLink
http://oncolink.upenn.edu

**Institute of Cancer Research**
**http://www.icr.ac.uk**

**Assoc. of Cancer Online Resources**
http://cure.acor.org

**One Woman's Reconstruction**
**http://spice.mhv.net/~delaney**

**Community Breast Health Project**
http://www-med.stanford.edu/CBHP

**Dr. Susan Love's Breast Book**
by Dr. Susan Love
Addison-Wesley
ISBN:  0-201-40835-X, 1995

**Avon Breast Cancer Awareness Crusade**
http://avon.avon.com/showpage.asp?thepage=crusade

**Pat Murray: My Experience With Breast Cancer**
http://web.mit.edu/pamurray/www/artbc.html

**Examining Myself**
**By Musa Mayer**
**Faber and Faber**
**ISBN:  0-571-19828-7, 1993**

---

**The business that designed my web site at:**
http://members.aol.com/rcampb3422/index.html
**and that brings me lots of visitors on the World Wide Web:**

**ALG Designs**
**1062 Hollywood Avenue**
**Des Plaines, IL  60016**
**(847) 827-3831**
**ALG** Designs@aol.com
**URL:**  http://members.aol.com/algdesigns/Default.htm
**ALG Designs creates, maintains and provides global marketing through Internet technologies for premium internet sites.**

*Part 1*

*Trouble*

# Chapter 1

## The Day

Six years. That's how long Portia loved her boyfriend, Darryl. Six years. Five months ago, he broke her heart. It was late September. An orange glow went across the sky; it darkened with the descent of the sun. The air was crisp and cool -- a day filled with temperatures Portia called "Peppermint Weather". Darryl drove his compact to her house. As usual, she could hear him approaching as soon as he opened the car door. A rhythm and blues cut blared through the radio. Darryl didn't drive anywhere without the radio turned up loud. Portia hurried to the door. They had been having loud, heated disagreements. At the end of their arguments that often spilled deep into the night, she blamed herself for bringing disenchantment into their relationship. She begged him not to leave when he threatened her with solitude. It was her role in their romantic affair. To accept the blame. To always be the one who was wrong. She forgave him six weeks ago after she found out he ran her telephone bill up to more than three hundred dollars in one month. She forgave him two weeks ago after he struck her. She'd drifted off to sleep in front of the television while the pan of lasagna his mother baked him a day earlier warmed in the oven. Scent of thick smoke went up her nose before she stirred out of the nap and ran into the kitchen. It was too late. The lasagna was burned. The noodles had gone from brown to black on the top. The beef and cheese in the center was dry and hard.

Darryl walked through the front door while she was fanning out the kitchen. "Hey, Baby!" he said to her while he pulled off his jacket and hung it in her closet.

Portia was silent. Her heart raced.

"What's that I smell?" he asked rounding the corner and walking inside the kitchen.

She stood in front of the oven with the door closed.

He smiled at her. "Smells like something's burning."

"I-I. Honey, I'm sorry. I fell asleep."

He tried to walk around her, but she prevented him. "What's going on? You making me a surprise?"

She chuckled dryly. "Not exactly."

He stared at her blankly. "Portia."

She started shaking her head. "I didn't mean to. It was an accident. I didn't realize how tired I was. Mama always told me not to cook while I was sleepy. Said I could fall asleep and burn something." She looked at him softly. "I did."

"You did what?"

"I was getting your dinner ready."

"You should. That's what a woman's supposed to do. Ain't nothing wrong with that. So what if it has a little burnt on it. Most women today can't cook worth two cents anyway. I'm hungry. I'll eat it. Take it out of the oven. I'm hungry." He kissed her forehead. "It's okay if you burned it a little. You ain't no chef. We both know that, but you do try and I appreciate that." A second later he snapped his finger. "Oh. You know what." He went to the refrigerator. "You can just heat me up some of Mama's lasagna. Mama. Now she knows how to cook. She can tear up anybody's kitchen. That's a soul food cooking woman." He smiled at her. "You can eat some of it too if you want to. Mama doesn't care. She likes you." He stuck his head in the refrigerator. "Where's the lasagna? Didn't I put it in here on the second shelf?"

Her arms shook. "It's in the oven."

After he closed the refrigerator, he walked toward her with a scowl. "What?"

"I fell asleep, Darryl. I had a hard-hard case today. I was in court all day today. I didn't realize how tired I was."

"You burned my mama's lasagna?"

"I didn't mean to. It was an accident."

"You and your non-cooking self. You burned my mama's lasagna?"

"Honey, I was tired."

He shoved her away from the oven door. "Move out of the way. Let me see what you did. Didn't your mama teach you how to cook anything? You can't even heat food right, Ms. Intellect. Ms. Professional."

She stood next to the counter gazing at the floor.

Opening the oven door, he pulled the lasagna out. Smoke billowed off its top. Its blackened, crusty top taunted his desire for perfection, his longing to see everyone and everything in the world be just as he thought they ought to be. It was as if the burned lasagna showed him the limit of his power. If he couldn't stop his favorite dish from burning he pondered the many other things he was powerless to control. A second later he told himself Portia brought him to this harsh realization, and balling his hand, he turned and punched her in the face. "Damn you! You can't do anything right! Burned my Mama's lasagna! You can't do anything! Everything you do turns out bad!"

Portia was stoical.

Looking at her standing against the counter with her head bowed, her gaze pointing toward the floor, he told himself she was not repentant for what she had done. A successful attorney – he knew she believed in herself. She was intelligent and admired in the community. Because of her mother's work in the school system and her father's contributions to civil rights, he knew her family was a pillar on the South Side. He envied the way people called out to her when they were in public, the attention she garnered by merely walking into a room. "You burned my Mama's lasagna on purpose! You did it on purpose!" He slapped her across the face. "Wanted to show me where I stood with you, huh? Wanted to get back at me for using your phone."

"No. It was an accident."

"Yea." He walked away from her and circled the kitchen floor. A moment later he stood in front of her slapping her hard – fast. "You think you and your people are better than me and my family. Think me and my people are low class, not smart and looked up to like your people are."

She shielded her face with her hands. "No, Darryl. Baby, that's not true. I don't feel that way at all. No one in my family does. I came up on the South Side. You know that."

No longer striking her, he snarled, "But you sure don't live there anymore, do you? You and all your people – even your community leading daddy – got out as soon as you could. Probably hated every second you had to spend living on the South Side, living around real black people."

She wept softly.

"You ain't nothing. Think you're something because your mama teaches English. That ain't nothing. Anybody can teach a bunch of idiots how to read and write. Your mama ain't doing nothing special. And those marches and meetings your dad held. He didn't do half as much as the real leaders in the black community. Look through any history book. Your daddy ain't in none of them. Never will be. He didn't do nothing. He ain't about nothing." Walking away from her, he went into the living room.

She kneeled to the floor and cried.

It took her fifteen minutes to pull herself together. Push her hair off her face. Wipe the evidence of tears from her eyes. Touch and stroke at the tears until they blended in with her skin. Until they dried and showed no more. Sniff hard until mucus stopped dribbling out of her nose. Smooth her hands across the edges of her face, her forehead, her nose. Places where he struck her. She thanked God when her face stayed smooth all over. No bruises this time. Then she looked up.

"What are you doing?"

She turned and faced the sink. "Just wiping my face."

He pushed her when he walked to the refrigerator. "You cry so easily." He took out a beer. One swig later, he belched. "So?"

She glanced at him.

He chuckled. "Is your face all wiped off?"

She was silent.

"Be stuck up. See if I care."

She turned away from the sink and walked toward the edge of the kitchen.

"Where are you going? Just where are you going?"

"Into my room to lay down. I'm tired."

His voice went up. "And I've been working all day."

"Honey, I'm tired. I had a hard day."

"What? Walking back and forth in front of some stupid judge. You call that working? I've really been working. Busting my behind loading and unloading trucks all day. Driving from one side of the city to the other."

"I know you work hard, Darryl. I respect—"

"I don't need you to respect me. I don't need your respect."

"Honey, I wasn't saying that. I didn't mean it like that. It's just that I know you work hard. Harder than I do. I know you do. I don't work anywhere near as hard as you do. I know that."

"Well." He took another swig of his beer. "Act like it sometimes."

She walked toward him and wrapped her arms around his back. "I love you, Darryl. I didn't mean to burn your Mama's lasagna. I'm so sorry, so very, very sorry. Please forgive me."

He swallowed hard. "Well. Okay. All right. Everybody makes mistakes every now and then." He shook his finger at her. "But don't let that happen again. My mama doesn't get around the way she used to. Her pressure's up so much of the time. She put a lot of time into making that lasagna. I forgive you, but I'm gonna have to tell her what you did. You know she's going to ask how I enjoyed the lasagna she made just for me." He shook his head. "I can't lie to my mama. I have to tell her the truth. I'm just letting you know. Being fair. I'm gonna tell her you burned her lasagna. It's that plain and that simple. I have to do it."

She kissed him on the forehead. "Okay. I understand. I deserve it. I shouldn't have put it in the oven when I was tired. I wanted it to be piping hot when you walked through the front door. That's why I went ahead and put it in the oven, but I was wrong. I should have waited."

After he took another swig of his beer, he hugged and kissed her. "It's okay. It's all right. You screwed up, but I forgive you. It's okay."

When she followed him out of the kitchen, he turned. "Where are you going?"

"I told you I was going to bed to lay down and rest. I'm tired. I'm exhausted, Darryl."

He shook his head. "You ain't going nowhere. Un-un. Not until I get some dinner. You just take yourself right back inside that kitchen and cook me up some grub."

Darryl's order to cook dinner haunted her while she walked toward the front door. She told herself she'd made mistakes, trusted her girlfriends when they told her he was cheating early-on in their relationship. He always denied it and had two to three of his closest friends vouch for him. She told herself she was wrong to take her girlfriends' word over his, but this was different. She had to talk to him. In the last two years she was sure he hadn't cheated, but her sister Faye saw him with a tall, shapely Sista three nights ago. She couldn't let that go. She and her sisters had a bond no man had broken. They didn't create stories. They didn't work to destroy each other's relationships. Their love was deep, like a long, hallow well that reached far below the earth. They looked out for one another, protected each other. They were each other's best friend. And – she told herself, after working tirelessly to love him for six years, it was time she stopped accepting Darryl's promises. Time to stop crying her way through the night.

Before she reached the edge of the living room, he shoved his key inside the lock and pushed the door open. He didn't give her time to speak. He stomped across the floor and threw his set of her house keys across the sofa. Then he faced the door. On his way back outside he told her he didn't love her anymore.

"Bu-But—" was the most she got out. When she went to bed that night, she cried herself to sleep.

Five months passed before she told herself she wanted to live. She had her father, Denny, to thank for rooting that desire in her heart. Since the day Darryl abandoned her love for him, her father told her stories about the early years he spent struggling to live, struggling to find someone to love, in Chicago.

She walked to her living room picture window and squinted. Thick fog clouded her vision. She smiled at the thought that her father, using his slow moving baritone voice, wanted to encourage her to gather her inner strength and move away from the pain the split with Darryl brought into her life.

While growing up, more times than she could count, she blurted, "I'm never going to fall in love or settle down," to her father. He had no reason to doubt her. She always showed herself to be a woman in control of her emotions and thoughts -- in control of her future.

She was the woman who stood in front of her bedroom mirror before the start of her menstrual cycle and vowed, "I'm gonna change. This spring, I'm gonna grow up."

Denny was walking by. He was carrying his work boots from a corner of the living room to his bedroom closet. His pace slowed when he heard her talking to her reflection in the mirror. He smiled at her back while he entered her bedroom.

When he neared her side, he asked her, "Who are you talking to, Miss?" Then he told her, "You're a good girl. Don't be so serious. Have a little fun. It's okay to be mischievous every now and then. Your mama and I don't make a big deal out of the playful things you do." He grinned. "Although we would appreciate it if you would stop picking those apples off of mean ol' Miss Barnes' tree." Though he tried not to, when he imagined Miss Barnes banging on the front door to tell him, "Portia's done gone and done it again! In a week, she done went and picked my tree clean!" he laughed.

He backed away from her. "Don't be in such a hurry to grow up," was the last thing he said to her before he crossed the hall and entered his own bedroom.

Portia was ten years old then. That spring, she did change.

She raced to the bathroom to pee one day after school. When she looked inside her panties, she saw sprinkles of blood. She stuck her head out the bathroom door and called for her mother. Two minutes later, her mother called Denny and sent him to the store. It wasn't long before Portia went into her dresser and pulled out a clean pair of cotton panties. She opened the bag Denny brought home from the store and slid a thick sanitary napkin onto the crotch of her underwear.

Four years later, when her hips starting spreading and thickening and swinging, she chewed on her bottom lip and told her father, "Just because I'm getting fat doesn't mean I like boys. I never liked a boy, and I never will. I don't need anybody. I'm strong. I can take care of myself." Two years passed before she stopped telling her father that. It was the same day she kissed Jerome Poindexter after he drove her home. They'd gone to a movie. She was a sophomore in high school.

Portia gazed out the window. Not one car headlight brightened the darkness outside her window. She stared into the night and thought about the changes her body and her life endured.

The wind shook the tree in her front yard until one of its branches broke. While she watched the branch fall to the ground, she wondered why she ever fell in love with Darryl. It went against her upbringing. Darryl was abusive. Her father never struck or screamed at her mother.

She was so much like her father. They both were thinkers. They both guarded their heart. Masked their deepest wants. Hid their emotions.

A hard wind rattled and shook the window. She crossed her arms and smiled softly. Despite her "I'm strong. I'm independent" pledges, she was glad her father knew when she needed him. She thought about the stories he told her during the last five months.

At the start of his stories, he was always riding a train that moved North away from Selma, Alabama -- and nightriders, house burnings and America's strange fruit. She still had the two brown, tatter-edged suitcases he climbed off that train with forty years ago.

"Here. Keep these." That's all he said at the end of his hour long visit four months ago while he pushed the two suitcases to the back of her living room closet. As soon as he walked away from her house and scooted behind the steering wheel of his silver Chevy, she hurried to the closet and pulled the suitcases out. She opened them so fast one of the tarnished clasps broke.

Inside the suitcases, she was surprised to find newspaper articles and magazine clippings that centered around Chicago's Riot of 1968 and four old black history books she remembered her parents reading to her and her siblings when she was a little girl. That afternoon four months ago, she scanned the newspaper articles and magazine clippings several times. Though the print in the articles said so, she couldn't recall her father being in jail for leading a civil rights march from the South Side to the mayor's house. "It was hard back then." That's all she said, her eyes misty, her brow wide, after she read the articles.

She dug deeper inside one of the suitcases and pulled out her father's dusty journal. Its pages were tarnished and turned up at the edges. The first entry read: "I've been here five weeks and every day all I've had to eat is dry toast for breakfast, lunch and dinner. Gotta get a job." She scanned down the journal and saw an asterisk. She smiled when she read the entry next to the asterisk. "October 12, 1945. I finally got a job at Boiling Automotive as an assembly line worker."

She turned her cloaked back to the picture window and looked at her living room. It was nothing like the living room her father described in his journal. She knew she was a long way from the leaky-roof, one room flat he called home in 1945. When she turned her gaze toward her living room's cathedral ceiling, she imagined leaves blowing off trees and dancing to the ground outside her father's one room flat. More than once, he told her the only furniture in the flat was a mildewed sofa that drooped in its middle where too many people sat for too long, and a splintered rocking chair. Yet, when he raised the window and listened to leaves crunch while Chicagoans living on the South Side walked on them, he believed the world pushed success into all his future days, days spent loving people in Chicago. It wasn't three years after he started welding dashboards, radios and horn buttons inside sedans and station wagons that he married her mama, Rebecca Armstrong.

She hung her head. She could still hear her father telling her, "Time flew after your mother and I got married at Mount Zion Baptist Church in 1947. Lord, after that, it wasn't long before we stood in front of you kids reading those thick black history books. Your brothers and sisters begged us not to read those books. We paid them no mind. We read all about Frederick Douglass, Sojourner Truth, Crispus Attacks and Harriett Tubman to all seven of you children -- every Wednesday we did. You ate it up. Every word. I could see your eyes begging for more while your mother and I read from those books."

The words older than a decade, Portia still knew her father spoke the truth. She did love to read, especially literature. She guessed the long hours she spent reading to be a reason Darryl and her relationship fell apart. Darryl always did complain that she didn't pay enough attention to him. He accused her of being too conservative. "You don't know how to have a good time." Whether they went to the movies, to a concert or out to eat, when he drove her home those were the first words out of his mouth.

"I'm not a social butterfly. I told you that the first time you asked me out. I'm a good woman though." She'd chuckle. Met with silence, she would add, "Don't I treat you right?"

"You do all right."

"All right?" Hours she spent washing, drying and ironing his clothes. Thousands of dollars she loaned him to meet bills (money he not once repaid her). The many times she turned and looked the other way during the first years of their relationship when he cheated on her. The lies she told her physician when she visited her office requesting salve for a new bruise. It all raced through her mind. "All right?"

"You don't like to party. I can't get you inside a club. Sometimes I think you're scared to let your hair down. Have fun. Live."

"I'm not scared to enjoy life. I have a loving family and the best friends any woman could want. I don't like to drin—"

"What are you trying to say?"

"Nothing, Darryl. I'm proud of the way you've been trying to stop drinking."

"Well. Whatever. Just don't get on no superior kick. You ain't an ounce better than me. Never will be."

"Why was I so bent on making him care about me? He never loved me." Swallowing a lump of emotion, she blinked hard. A second later, she raised then lowered her shoulders with a sigh. Despite her loyalty and affection toward him, she told herself Darryl was right. She told herself she didn't pay enough attention to him. She told herself she was too rigid, a perfectionist. A woman out of touch with her emotions. Staid. She told herself she didn't know how to love a man. Now here she was standing in front of her living room window trying to decide if she should go to *The Chronicle's* Christmas party, an annual event she hadn't missed since she bought her house ten years ago.

It was 1982. The leaves that were on the ground when Darryl spit, "I don't love you anymore!" at her didn't show themselves when she looked out her window. It was cold outside. The leaves were covered with snow.

It took her two hours to decide to stop pacing the floor -- going from the picture window to the sofa back to the picture window. After she pulled on her ankle-length leather coat, she reached to the back of the living room closet for her purse. The streets were quiet while she drove to the party. This was the first time she'd gone alone. She kept looking in the rearview mirror at her hair, her eyeliner, her lipstick. She wanted to look beautiful, but she kept finding a spot where her make-up was smudged.

"Oh, well," she said while she pulled into the parking lot. "I look all right."

The party was crowded. Except for a few couples she saw when she entered the room, faces at the party were new to her. She spent the night twirling and refreshing her glass of orange juice until her eyes fell across the ebony skin of a tall, broad shouldered man's smooth face. She learned what his name was by being nosy.

"Girl, Dennis is fine," a tall, slender Sista said with a wave of her hand. Her girlfriend, equally as slim, leaned forward and clung to her every word. "He has a nice house out by The Hub. He has a Bachelor's Degree in Biology, and a Master's Degree in Chemistry. In fact, he's teaching a Master's level Chemistry course at Chicago University. And, Girl," Portia followed the woman's gaze while it crossed over Dennis' face, shoulders and thighs, "He's available."

It was midnight when she gathered her courage and introduced herself to Dennis. Her hands shook. Her voice cracked. "Hi. I'm Portia. I couldn't help but notice you from across the room."

Dennis smiled at her nervousness.

Twenty minutes into their conversation, she learned that he loved children, weight lifting, running in early Saturday morning 10K road races and hiking. She learned that he was an only child, but, he was careful to tell her, "I'm not spoiled. I mean, yes. I was an only child, but my mother was a single parent. She worked forty hours a week as a city college clerk. I don't think she ever made more than eight thousand dollars a year. We didn't have a lot of luxuries."

He pushed fire beneath her skin when he looked inside her eyes. While he talked, she thought about how not once during the party did she see him fondle a glass of liquor. She couldn't help but smile. A man drinking didn't escape her. Darryl saw to that. After living through six screaming years of his alcohol induced rages, she vowed to never love a man who drank again.

Dennis made her laugh. A deep, rolling chuckle raced out of his chest when he told her, "Two years ago while I was on my way to work at the university, I was in this car accident. Right. A cop rear-ended me. I was laid up in the hospital for two months after that cop ran into me. Lord, I never thought there were so many lawyers in Chicago pulling for a Brother until that accident. I think every law firm in Chicago contacted me. They wanted to know if I wanted to sue the city. It got so bad at one point, to throw the lawyers off the scent of long money, I thought Chicago University's medical staff was going to have to ship me out of the state to some unknown hospital until my back healed and I got on my feet again."

A civil court case attorney with six years experience at Courtney & Sons, a downtown law firm, an attorney who never had fewer than four cases a month, Portia's short Afro was turning gray. Dennis' humor worked like magic to take her thoughts away from work -- to heal her broken heart.

***

"Dennis," Portia called on a night two years into their relationship. "It's not too cold outside. Let's go jogging on the bike trail at the park close to your house."

"All right," he said while he pushed his way off her sofa. An hour later, he labored to catch his breath while he pulled off his hooded sweat suit at the side of her bed.

He ran his hands over the top of his Afro. "I need a shower."

Portia stood in front of her bedroom mirror picking her Afro. "You know where the towels and wash rags are. After you come out of the bathroom, I'm going to get in there and take a long, hot bath."

"What do you want for dinner?" he called before he closed the bathroom door. He already knew what she would answer. He knew she would suggest The Trudor, a steak and ale restaurant, Dale's Fish and Chips, or Swanks, a jazz club that served the best fettucini this side of heaven.

She laid the pick on her dresser and patted the top of her Afro. "Let's go to Swanks."

The following evening, as if good food wasn't enough to season a relationship with, after she backed her BMW out of Courtney & Sons' parking lot at 6:00, Portia drove to the Miriam Theatre. She told the lady working the box office to give her two of the best front row seats the theatre had so Dennis and she could catch "A Raisin In The Sun" while it toured Chicago.

That night, Dennis wasn't at her house when she drove her BMW up the side driveway. For that, she was glad. She raced inside her house. After she closed the door, she went straightway to the telephone. She dialed 555-2222 and waited for a familiar voice to answer.

"Hello?" The lady on the other line said.

"Hi, Patty!" Portia enthused into the receiver. "It's Portia."

"Hey, Girl. I know what you want. You're spoiling that man. It's not even a holiday." Patty clucked her tongue then she chuckled. "What are you going to send that gorgeous man of yours now?"

Portia grinned at the receiver. "Can I get an assortment of tulips, lilacs or yellow and white carnations? And, oh," she dug through the mouth of her purse for her gold Master Card. "I want the gift card to read -- Dennis, you mean so much to me. I love you with all my heart -- Portia."

Patty, owner of Tiffany's Flowers, a small shop that wired and shipped floral arrangements across the country answered, "You got it."

Portia hung up the telephone and waited for Dennis to come through the front door. She didn't have to wait long. She was sitting at her dining room table sipping hot, apple cinnamon tea when he pushed his key inside the lock in her front door.

"Hey, Baby," he called out before he crossed the living room floor and reached her side.

"Hey," she called back. "If you're not too tired, do you want to read some of Countee Cullen's poetry later tonight? We can order Chinese and eat while I read."

He kissed her mouth with longing before he answered, "Yes. I'd like that."

"Dennis?"

He watched her push her tea toward the center of the table. "Yes?"

"You're so good to me."

Pulling a chair out, he sat next to her. "Good is the only way for a man to treat a woman like you." He reached for her hand and kissed it.

Her gaze lowered, "I don't know. No one's ever been this good to me." She looked up. "Sometimes I get scared."

"Scared? Scared of what?'

"That it won't last. That something will happen. That you won't always love me."

"Portia," he cupped her chin with his palm. "I'm never going to stop loving you. Sure. They'll be ups and downs, but nothing's going to come between us. I knew that the first time I laid eyes on you."

"You were watching me?" She grinned. "At the party?"

"Oh. I saw you all right. Spotted you as soon as you walked through the door."

"And you let me sit by myself all that time?"

"When I saw you talking to those couples, I thought you knew who was who. Thought I was the stranger at the party. That was my first time there."

"It's not like it used to be. When I started going to *The Chronicle*'s annual Christmas get-together, there were mainly only couples at the party. Now I see so many single folk there. It's getting to be like a club gathering and I've never liked cl-- Well. I'm not a big party type. Not that you couldn't tell."

"I had a lot of fun with you after you got up the nerve to introduce yourself to me."

"Glad I did, seeing as you weren't making your way toward me that night."

"Portia, you're so fine, I was sure you were taken."

She blushed. "No."

"He was a fool."

She chuckled.

"He was. Letting you go."

"No. I was the fool. For not letting him go sooner."

They leaned back in their chairs and laughed.

Portia stopped laughing and caught her breath. She stared at Dennis. "Your eyes. The way they squint when you laugh hard. You look so much like my father when your eyes squint like that."

"You're crazy about your dad, aren't you?"

"Yeah. He's my twin, or, I'm his twin – I should say."

"I like your dad. He's cool. Your family is good people."

"Thanks." She lowered her voice. "Dennis?"

"Yes?"

"I want to ask you something. Please let me know if it's too painful to answer. If it is, I'll leave it alone."

"No." He moved to the edge of his chair and looked at her intently. "Go ahead."

"Why don't you ever talk about your father?"

"Because I don't really know him." He shrugged. "I really don't. He left when I was two or three years old. I was still wobbling around, just a toddler. My mom said he just packed his bags one day and walked out the front door. Never said good-bye, hugged or kissed me or anything. Just walked out the door and never looked back."

"I admire the way your mother raised you by herself. She did an excellent job. I know it must have been hard for her."

"She never complained. There were times when I sensed money was tight or that she was tired, but not once did she complain. She didn't put my dad down or walk around feeling sorry for herself. You see how she is. My mom goes with the flow. She's focused. She knows what she wants to get out of life. She's all about family, always has been. When I was coming up, I hardly ever heard her holler. The few times she did holler at me, I deserved it. I was a hard headed somebody when I was a kid. My mom. She's a very peaceful woman."

"Not at all like her mother."

They laughed again.

"You're grandmother is something."

"She sure is. She helped raise me. I stayed with her while my mom was working. I did not cross my grandmother. She was good with a peeled switch."

"How did your mother do it? Did she ever want to get married again?"

"Oh. She dated, but every man she met reminded her too much of my father. She always found a reason to call it off. I don't think she'll ever get serious with a man again. Wish she would, but I don't think that's gonna happen. She's happy with her garden, and Gran still lives with her. Those two are like Siamese twins. Inseparable."

"Even when you think you're alone, you never are."

"I never saw it that way, but, yeah. You're right. In fact, those two are going on a mad shopping spree this weekend."

"What?"

"Can you believe they tried to get me to go?"

"They must be out of their minds."

He chuckled. "You got that right."

"You're an on-time man, Dennis, but you don't like to shop. I mean, really shop. Look around and take your time nad shop."

"Remember that time I flew you and your sister Deborah to Paris?"

"Child."

"How many times did you call me?'

"I should have just given you a list and let you go."

"How many times did you call me, Portia?'

"I don't know. A hundred times."

"More like a thousand."

She laughed. "Deborah and I walked in more circles. We were lost for what had to be more than half of our first day in Paris."

"And still came back with bags and bags and bags of clothes."

"We had a blast once we learned how to get around. Those hand drawn maps you faxed me did the trick. The way you drew those maps, a person would think you were born and raised in Paris."

He chuckled. "Guess what?"

"What?"

"I only know my way around the shopping areas. I flew my mom and grandma there a little over two years ago. Just a little before I met you." He winked at her. "My grandma always walked around talking about how my grandfather promised to take her to Paris. After he died she kept talking about wanting to go. She talked it up until my mom started saying she wanted to go too. So one day I decided to save up my money and fly all three of us to Paris. We stayed for a week." He laughed. "My grandma tried every kinda food, every kinda drink. I didn't think I was going to be able to drag her back on that plane."

"I don't blame your grandmother. Paris is a place I will never forget. Deborah and I took so many pictures while we where there. After all those pictures I showed you, do you know I still have two rolls of film I haven't developed from that trip?"

Next time it's you and me."

"What were you doing then? What kept you away? Kept you from going? I forgot."

"Remember? Classes. Finals. Dean wouldn't let me out of that one for nothing. When I bought those tickets, finals was the last thing on my mind. When I looked at my calendar and saw the date for finals, I was sick."

"Next trip to Paris is my treat. We can go Paris and act like lovers do."

Pulling her close, he whispered, "We can stay right here and act like lovers do."

He took her hand inside his and guided her to the sofa. "Stay right there."

She watched him cross the floor. "Where are you going?"

"How about some Quiet Storm?" A second later, Barry White was crooning on the stereo.

He stepped away from the stereo and rounded the corner.

"Now where are you going?"

"I'll be right back."

He returned to the room carrying two crystal goblets and a bottle of red wine.

Uncrossing her legs, she smiled and blew him a slow kiss.

After he placed the goblets on the coffee table in front of the sofa and filled them with the cold wine, he sat next to her. He pulled her close. They raised their glasses and he toasted her with, "To forever."

Late that night, the moon shined in the sky. Portia closed the book of poetry, placed it on a corner of her nightstand then told Dennis to 'roll over'. She climbed atop his stomach and reached to her nightstand. She grabbed a bottle of coconut oil. After she kissed Dennis' mouth, she saturated her fingers with the lubricant. She leaned across his long, trim body. She pushed and pulled her fingers over his thighs, stomach, back and chest. His chest hair slid between her fingers. She didn't stop moving her hands over his body until the ends of her fingers tingled, his shoulders and neck were free of tension, and the scent of oil billowed from her bed covers to the ceiling. "I love you," came away from her mouth before she tucked her shoulders into his and fell into a deep sleep.

Outside her bedroom window, the tree in her front yard budded. Tucked inside Dennis' love, she dreamed herself inside a lacy, white wedding gown. She smiled into the night when she dreamed the long aisle of Mount Zion Baptist Church into view. She slept long and peacefully.

The only thing she had left to do before she became Dennis' wife was to visit her physician, Dr. Kirnan. She had to have her blood drawn to complete the medical portion of her wedding license. Since her annual check-up was only one month away, earlier in the day when she telephoned Dr. Kirnan's office, she told Kathy, the receptionist, to, "Oh, just go ahead and put me down for a pap and a breast exam too when I come in to have my blood drawn."

## Chapter 2

## A Crying Season

Portia placed her purple straw clutch purse on the bureau. Her Aunt Lillian gave her the purse Thursday for her 28th birthday. She scanned the top of the bureau. She hoped to find a note from Dennis. She smiled when she thought about how she had been her Aunt Lillian's favorite niece since she was two years old.

It was her Aunt Lillian who pulled her atop her lap and sang, in a broken, alto voice, "Hush brown sugar. Don't you cry. Auntie Lillie's gonna buy you a diamond ring. And if the check she buys it with bounces, she's gonna take that ugly ring back to the store and buy you a pack of bubble gum. The kind wrapped in paper with cartoons on it."

If uncertainty weren't filling her thoughts, she would laugh at the words to the song her Aunt Lillian sang to her twenty-three years ago. She was visiting her parents' with her gold-toothed boyfriend.

She was outside crying when her aunt walked through her parents' front door. She'd fallen and busted her knees. But that wasn't the reason she cried. Tears came away from her eyes and "huh-huh-huh" came away from her heaving breasts because she lost her favorite doll. It was a black china doll. Its hair was shiny and curly -- just like Portia's. Its eyes were dark brown and big -- just like Portia's. Its mouth was small and more pink than red -- just like Portia's. Its face always wore a grin. It was a happy doll just like Portia was a happy little black girl -- happy until she lost her pretty, black china doll.

As soon as she saw her aunt's car, she raced inside the house. She ran to her crying, "I-I-I lost Sister. I-I-I lost my Sister doll." She didn't grin again until her aunt sang her the fixed-up version of Hush Little Baby. Two days later when her aunt drove to her parents' house with a new gold-toothed man at her side, Portia laughed and jumped. Her aunt kissed her forehead and pushed a brand new black china doll inside her arms.

Finished with the search, Portia frowned. The bureau top was bare.

Exhaustion sent one side of her face down when she pushed her left shoe off. She spent too much of her day walking. Hard corns on the outside of her smallest toes caught in her stockings. A raw ache stabbed the sides of her feet. She stopped moving and grimaced.

Her house keys clanged when they hit the top of the bureau. They fell next to her purse. Two tickets she purchased for Dennis and her to attend Saturday evenings Earth, Wind and Fire concert spilled out of the mouth of the purse. She leaned forward and rested her elbows against the top edge of the bureau. The afternoon having sent a crisis into her life, she hoped she hadn't purchased the tickets too soon.

She turned a pink telephone message in her hand. She stared at the numbers scribbled across its front. She didn't stop looking at the numbers until she pulled one of her dining room chairs away from the table and sat down. She picked up the telephone and dialed 555-2244.

"Hello?"

"Yes." She crossed her legs and pulled on her blouse collar. "Is Dr. Kirnan there?"

A long sigh went out of the nurse's mouth. "May I ask who's calling please?"

"Por--"

"Oh. Portia." The nurse's voice went up. "Portia Fowler!"

"Ye-Yes." Portia pulled the receiver closer to her ear. "Hi, Linda. Ah -- I had tests performed nearly three weeks ago. Dr. Kirnan left me a message at work that my results were in. He said it was very important. I was at lunch when he called."

"Hang on. Let me get your medical record out of the file."

"Linda?"

"Yes?"

"Why are you answering the phone?"

"Besides Dr. Kirnan, I'm here all by myself. Kathy went to get us something to eat."

Portia ran her fingers through her hair. "Late night tonight, huh?"

"Yes. I'm covering the phones while Kathy's away. You know answering telephones isn't my repertoire."

Portia twisted the collar of her blouse and chuckled dryly. "You home from court already?"

She swung her shoeless foot across the floor. "I don't go to court every day. I left the firm early today." She ran her hand back and forth across her brow.

"Good. You should rest now and then." She dug through the file cabinet, "Okay. Portia, let me just—"

Portia swallowed hard. "How's your son? He was in the office the last time I was there. Your husband and he were stopping in to give you something. Your son has gotten so big."

"Yes. He's growing up." She opened Portia's file. "Portia, let me—"

Portia turned her feet over. "You and your husband make such a happy couple. I always like seeing you two together."

Linda smiled while she wondered why Portia was being so chatty. "Thank you. Aren't you getting married soon?"

After she wiped sweat off her forehead, Portia chuckled. She thought about the time when the firm discussed changing HMO carriers. She refused to switch doctors. If she had to pay monthly health care expenses out of her own pocketbook to keep Dr. Kirnan as her primary physician, she would. After being his patient since the day she was born, she knew no other doctor's office would embrace her with warmth and friendship the way Dr. Kirnan and his staff did.

She cleared her throat. "I'm waiting on my test results."

Linda took Portia's medical record out of the file. She scanned it before she returned her attention to the telephone. Her eyes ballooned. She pulled the receiver against her mouth and said, "Portia. Hold on. Let me get Dr. Kirnan. He's in the back in his office going through charts."

Portia stiffened her spine and chewed on her bottom lip. "What-does-it-say?"

"Now you know I can't tell you that. But, you know whatever your record says, we're going to take good care of you." She read Dr. Kirnan's scribble hurriedly. "Like you told me, it says here that Dr. Kirnan wants to talk with you today. Let me buzz him and let him know you're on the line."

Portia twirled her blouse collar between two of her fingers until she heard Dr. Kirnan's deep voice cross the wire.

"Portia. Portia?"

Moving to the back of the dining room chair, she arched her brow and pulled the receiver closer to her mouth. "Hello, Dr. Kirnan."

After he placed a chart on his desk, Dr. Kirnan smiled. "Hey, kid. I'm glad you returned my call. Thank you. How was work?"

She stiffened her upper lip. "Okay."

"Good. Well." He ran his hand across his brow and sighed. "Portia, I have good news and bad news. What do you say we start with the bad news so we can work steadily up to the good news?"

She cleared her throat before she answered, "Sure."

"As yo--Are you sitting down?"

"Yes."

"Good." He paused and gave Linda a nod of thank you for placing Portia's medical record in front of him on his desk. "As you know, after we discovered the lump in your left breast approximately three weeks ago, I scheduled you for a mammogram, an ultrasound and a biopsy. We've covered a lot of bases. The bad news is, the lump is malignant. It's the size of a bean. The good news is, we can work to heal your body using a local treatment. I'm going to give you some therapies we can use to rid your body of this tumor. Although I'm your physician, this is your body we are talking about. I want you to take at least a week to make a decision. You tell me what form of treatment you prefer. We can talk for as long as you want. I'll answer every question you have. For every question I can't answer, I'll find an answer and get back to you right away. All right?"

She answered with silence.

To which he responded, "Portia? You all right?"

Nodding in quick jerks, she whispered, "Yes. Yes. Yes, I'm all right."

"You don't have to be, especially now. But if you are -- I'll continue."

She nodded again. "Go ahead."

When she returned the receiver to its cradle, she placed her head between her hands. Her face tightened and loosened in spasms. The room felt hot. She thought about opening a window or going outside. She lowered her hands when she felt her eyes fill with tears.

Away from her face, her hands balled into fists. She swallowed hard and straightened her spine the same way she saw her mother sit when her father was jailed at the height of the Civil Rights Movement when she was a little girl. She sat still in the silence until words came to her. They bore her mother's voice. "Life is no easy trick, but give up is something Fowler's simply don't do." She raised her hands and placed them over her eyes, as if by not being able to see, she could erase the pain. "Do you know how many times I've wanted to quit? Thought about just giving up?" She sniffed and made a half-hearted attempt to count the many times she heard her mother say that while she was a little girl sitting next to her on the sofa. Home for them was the projects. It was always dark outside when Portia treated herself to the warmth of her mother's resting body. A rare treat. Rebecca was a busy woman with tight deadlines to meet. Those nights they sat on the sofa together and waited for Denny to walk through the front door. While her siblings played in their bedrooms upstairs, Portia kept her mother company. She sensed her mother's fear. Her longing to see Denny . . . with her . . . with their family. Off the streets. Away from marches, angry police officers, bigots and madmen. But it never happened, even years after the Reverend Dr. Martin Luther King Jr. was assassinated. Denny took to the streets in a quest for justice. For this Portia admired him. Howbeit waiting for her father to come home created a deep fear in her. She grew accustomed to sitting at home waiting for a good man to walk through the front door.

The storm door opened. At once, Portia's memories were broken by the sound of approaching footsteps. She stood from the dining room table.

Taking long strides, she went into the living room. At the edge of the room, she chewed on her bottom lip and walked toward the first man in her life outside her father she knew beyond her fears, beyond each of her doubts, loved her -- her.

Dennis smiled across the living room at her. "Hi."

A yellow knit shirt clung to his arms. The pair of loose fitting jeans and the pair of blue and white sneakers he wore told her that he stopped off at home before he came to see her. She smiled hard. "Hi."

"How did everything go today?"

She extended her arms and created a T out of the top portion of her body. "Okay. How was your day? How did your students do on their exams?" She let out a deep breath, dropped her arms to her sides and examined the lines crossing his forehead. "What's wrong?"

He narrowed his brow. "I was going to ask you that."

She stepped back. She cautioned herself to smile. She knew a smile would camouflage her rising anger. "Can't I ask how your students did on the exam without something being wrong with me?"

His gaze traveled above her crossed arms. He looked at her with intent. "I think the results of your biopsy and blood work is more important. I mean. Didn't you tell me Dr. Kirnan was supposed to call you with the results today?"

She threw her head back, and worked a scowl all around her mouth. Her arms went against her breasts so hard, it startled her, "I might have said that. I don't remember every thing I say."

He nodded before he let out a deep breath. "Portia, why are you acting like there's nothing to talk about? Why are you putting off facing this?"

Uncrossing her arms and digging the scowl into her face until her brow furrowed, she turned her back against his stare. She walked toward her bedroom. Then, with a click of her heel, she jerked her shoulders and stomped toward the kitchen. Dennis followed her.

The saloon-style kitchen doors swished on their brackets when she pushed them. Near the edge of her glass top kitchen table, she slowed her steps. She listened to her low-heeled dress shoe click tip-tip-tap across the linoleum floor.

A second later, she pressed her palms down on the kitchen table and turned. She stood gape-eyed while she faced the counter that separated the stove and the refrigerator. She pulled her other low-heeled dress shoe off. She watched the shoe tumble to its side.

Dennis crossed the floor and shortened the distance that separated them. "There you go chewing on your lip."

She glared at him and slapped the table. "You know I'm angry, don't you?" She clenched her teeth. "You think you know everything about me."

"No. No. I don't think I know everything about you. You're too deep a woman, too interesting a woman, for me or anyone to be able to know everything about you." He shook his head from side to side as if he was trying to cut her rage in half. "I do know you're hurting."

She thought her arms crossed all on their own. "You take pride in knowing me well."

He raised his hand and turned its palm toward her. "No, Portia. Now. Come on."

"No." She stepped back and threw her hand down to her side. Two warm tears came away from her eyes. They took their time getting down her face.

"Come on. Stop."

She dragged her feet across the floor until the crown of her head reached below the bottom of his chin. "That was Dr. Kirnan's office! My test results are in! You can forget about how special you always say I am because I'm so different from everybody else! How I do and say what I want, not what I think everybody wants me to do or say! Forget it! Forget it! Not even ten minutes ago, I found out that I'm a one in eight American woman." She threw her head back. "That's right! I have breast cancer!" That said, more words came to her than she thought she had room for on her tongue -- angry, loud words -- soaked in pain. "I've had the malignant tumor in my left breast for ten years!"

He stepped back. "Ten years?"

"Most tumors don't grow just-like-that, Dennis! It takes years for a lump to form in a woman's breast." She chewed on her bottom lip. "And I thought I was saving my life all those times I examined my breasts after I took a shower."

His brow went up. "What?"

"Ten years, Dennis. What! Are you deaf? I said it usually takes years for cancer to grow into the size lump a woman can feel. Most lumps don't even show up on mammograms as soon as they form."

"How do you know all of this?"

She chewed her bottom lip. "Dr. Kirnan just told me." She raised her hands. When they came down, her face washed with tears. Every thing around her moved slow, almost stopped. The confession seemed more a half death than a spoken, a shared, truth. Hearing her voice run, loud and rocky, she cautioned herself not to deliver a jeremiad.

"Dr. Kirnan said I have a lump the size of a bean. Since I've already had a mammogram, an ultrasound and a biopsy, I told him to go ahead and schedule me for a lumpectomy. He wanted me to wait and think about it, but I said 'no'. He thinks the surgery coupled with radiation treatments will rid my body of cancer."

Dennis' eyes ballooned. "What is a lumpectomy?"

She talked through clenched teeth. "They remove the tumor, not the entire breast!" She turned her back to him. "Do I have to explain all this to you! I just found out myself!"

He folded his arms and sighed. "I'm asking because I care." Then he narrowed his brow and raised his voice. "Are you sure this lumpectomy will cure you? I mean, what if it doesn't get it all?"

Moving as slow as a doll on a china stand, she turned and faced him. "Who are you? You're going to tell me what I need? I don't want a doctor cutting my whole breast away from me! Not too many doctors perform lumpectomies, but Dr. Kirnan told me he's fairly certain it'll work." She tossed her hands into the air. "I'm taking the chance." Then she tightened her brow and stared down the bridge of her nose at Dennis. "And cure." She chuckled dryly. "Cure? Cure. Cure! There ain't no cure!" She raised her voice until veins at the sides of her head pumped. "And I'm not going to Atlantic City with you this summer! I'm not walking behind all those pretty women in their little bikinis while they sashay in front of you men." She shook her head. "No. Un-un. Not after I've been cut on."

"Por--"

"And don't you go calling your mother and asking her a bunch of stupid questions. She never had breast cancer. She can't tell you how I feel!"

"Now, Por--"

"And don't hang around me pretending that you really love me when all you do is feel sorry for me either. Go on." She shooed him away from her with the side of her hand. "Go on. Go get yourself one of those fine women. Go get yourself a woman who doesn't have to be cut on, a woman who doesn't have to live the rest of her life knowing she has breast cancer."

"Please! Would yo--"

"Don't think you have to stay with me. I can manage just fine without you. I don't need a man in my life. You don't have to love me if you don't want to." Her gaze rolled down to her blouse collar, to her hands, to her knees, to her feet, to the floor. When her gaze climbed again to Dennis' brow, tears wetting her face slowed. "What am I crying about? It's always something with me. I get one good thing and lose another. It's always been that way with me." Her throat tightened. She swallowed hard. "Every time I think I'm going to break up, break into a million little pieces, somebody rescues me -- and all that happens is . . ." She spread her hands. Her shoulders heaved. "I get knocked down again."

Dennis' shoulders went up. "Come here."

She pushed back, out of the reach of his extended arms. "That's the most you can do? You can't cry? You can't grieve with me?"

"Portia, you know we've talked about this before. We've known about this since you had your annual check-up -- what? Three weeks ago. You'll beat this. We both know that. Early detection can only help. It's better that you found out now rather than two years from now. You've done the right thing. You'll beat this. This isn't going to last forever."

"That changes things?" She took another step backwards. "It's so like you to think knowledge changes every thing!"

He softened his voice. "Come here."

*Part 2*

*Bridges*

# Chapter 3

## *Family*

Portia looked at Dennis and wondered how he would react if it was his mother telling him she had breast cancer -- his mother instead of her. She knew how close he was to his mother. He telephoned her three to four times a week. He talked about her what seemed to Portia like everyday.

Unlike his father, who hadn't telephoned, written or visited since he stomped out of the house when Dennis was only three years old, Dennis told her that his mother never hurt him, never let him down, not once betrayed his trust. She guessed his love for his mother was the reason he paid so much attention to her. He seemed born with the wisdom to know what it took to please a woman. He always gave her a back rub and ran her a tub of hot, bubble bath when she told him she was tired from spending ten grueling hours in court. When his friends rang his house and asked him to go to a game, a concert or to watch a big boxing match on TV with them, if Portia and he already had a scheduled date, he told his friends he'd catch them later. Although not an avid church-goer, he respected Portia's beliefs and spiritual principles. "I believe in God. Don't doubt that for a minute." He assured her. "Guess I'm going through a period where I don't agree with a lot that I see happening in churches. I know I have to deal with it, and I am. I'm dealing with it. I'm trusting God about this."

In the dead of winter, he shoveled Portia's BMW out of her side driveway and warmed the engine before she came outside to drive herself to church. When they socialized in large crowds and he sensed that she was feeling uncomfortable and shy, he moved close to her and told her jokes and funny stories until she laughed hard. He was warm and sincere. Clearly, she knew that he loved her even though he wasn't a man given to saying, "I love you" often.

In so many ways he was like her. He didn't wear his emotions on his sleeve. Until today, she regarded his caged emotions as a show of strength. He was nothing like Darryl, a man she thought she would never miss . . . until today.

If she had told Darryl, "I have breast cancer," he would have snatched her by the arm and rushed her to the nearest hospital emergency room. He would have pounded the waiting area counter and demanded of the staff, "Get up! Call yourself a hospital! One of you white coated idiots better get up and come see about my woman!"

She almost shook her head. No. She didn't miss Darryl. The six years they were together, he screamed at her more than he hugged her. He pushed her in public. He screamed obscenities at her when he was out of work and she told him she didn't have spare money to pay his rent. He ate her refrigerator empty and dirtied her house when he was drunk then accused her of lacking domestic skill. The way he embarrassed her and bruised her feelings with his harsh criticisms -- he didn't love her.

She belonged with Dennis. He knew how to love a woman.

She walked inside Dennis' arms, buried the side of her face against his chest and wept. While warm tears inched down her face, she thought about her father, the man who encouraged her to move her deepest emotions outside heartache, the man who encouraged her to fall in love again.

A community leader, that was her father. He never went along with an agenda just because it was popular. She was proud of the way he stood behind his beliefs, stood behind them with his life. Doing so cost him. She'd never forget the night he was jailed for standing up for what he believed in, for fighting for a better way of life. She loved him for the way he treated her mother, the way he protected his children like a far reaching umbrella keeps the rain out.

Dennis stroked the side of her face. Her tears fell against his hand like summer rain. "What are you thinking about?"

"My father."

"It won't be as hard on your parents as you think it will be. You already know they're going to stand by you.'

She sniffed. "I know. I know that. It's just that they've both already been through so much. Seems like my father has been fighting all his life. Stories he told me about growing up in Alabama. Marches during the 60s. He was in the middle of it all."

"He left you an excellent example of what it is to put up a good fight."

"I know," she said nodding. "I know. I just don't want to be the one to bring more pain, more heartache into his life."

"That's not what you're doing, Portia."

"Well, this certainly won't make him happy."

He chuckled dryly. "No. We both know tha—"

"Sorry. I was being sarcastic."

"You're frustrated. Those emotions are going to find someplace to go."

"I don't mean to point them at you. You don't deserve that."

"No, but I'd rather you talk and get your feelings out than hold the pain and confusion inside."

She pressed her head against his chest. "I love you so much. I'm just so scared." She chuckled.

"What's so funny?"

"I'm thinking about how scared I was when my dad didn't come home from work one night. He said he was going to a meeting after work. He never came home that night. Mama didn't know, but I spent the entire night sitting on the edge of my bed staring out the window, waiting for my dad to come up the sidewalk. I was grown before Mama told me what really happened." She chuckled again. "Before it was over, Dad made the paper." Wrapping her arms around Dennis, she let her memories take her back twenty years.

"Last night, charges of inciting a civil disturbance were leveled against seven men who marched a group of South Side residents to the mayor's house. The charges were dropped early this morning." Finished reading the article out loud to Rebecca, Denny cleared his throat and shook the evening newspaper. When he turned and looked at his wife, he saw her hips sway. He saw her hair, recently permed and curled at the ends, dip down to her shoulders. He stared at her stiffened spine and chuckled. Not one day out of their eighteen-year marriage had he seen her out of control.

It was dawn when the jailer pushed him toward a telephone. He called home and told Rebecca to phone their attorney. While he relayed the message, he sensed that fear was removed from her thoughts. In fact, more than the clink of the jailer's key opening his cell door an hour later, it was the sound of her voice that calmed him. She told him, "You did the right thing, Baby. You were right to march those folks to the mayor's house. It's time somebody forced the mayor to keep his campaign promises." The volume in her voice went up. "It's time the mayor ordered the transportation department to fill potholes in the streets out here. It's time the mayor directed a sanitation truck to service our neighborhoods before garbage goes blowing across people's front lawns. It's time the mayor drafted a proposal to have these vacant buildings boarded up and graffiti painted off the sides of the schools our children go to. No! You didn't do anything wrong. You did something that was long overdue." Then she lowered her voice and rid it of the anger that banked in it seconds ago. "I love you, Denny. I'm proud of you. I'll stay up until you get home. I'll wait up on the living room sofa."

Denny turned in the kitchen chair and listened to the sound of Rebecca's voice. Instead of hearing her calm his fears, he heard her calling their children in for dinner. "Robert! Craig! Edwin! Ressey! Deborah! Faye! Portia!" After she called her children, Rebecca turned from where she stood in front of the stove stirring creamy, white gravy. She rested her right hand on the thick of her spine and dropped her hips. Denny watched her back sway and knew she'd moved beyond her rage at his late night arrest. He looked at her furrowed brow and knew she was upset about having to holler to call their children inside the house. Sarcasm made its way into her voice. "Denny, will you call those kids in, please?"

Denny lay the newspaper on the table before he turned sideways in his chair and looked at her. "Baby, I know it's been rough with the city boycotts and my holding civil rights meetings at the community center, but the kids haven't done anything." When only silence came from her, he arched his brow and asked, "Woman, what's wrong with you?"

Turning the fire beneath the pan of gravy out, Rebecca walked across the room. She hushed her voice behind tightly pursed lips. She was silent with guilt while she stood over the sink staring out into the back yard. Forcing her to summon them twice before they came inside for dinner was usually the most her children did to try her patience. To quiet her guilt, she stared out the back window. A huddle of knotty headed children played freeze tag three apartment buildings down from the building she and her family lived in. She watched the chocolate children's bodies zig, zag, run, duck and freeze.

Propping her elbow against the edge of the sink, she smiled. The playing children made her think about her own childhood. She moved like the children in the back yard did when she was a little girl. Her sisters' laughter always accompanied her on those long ago afternoons. The sky was always clear, and the clouds looked as if they were floating aimlessly through the air.

Rebecca lowered her head. As it was with her, so it was with her own daughters. Portia, Ressey, Deborah and Faye never failed to form a quartet before they headed out the front door on Saturday mornings. A jump rope, a bag of jacks, or chalk for drawing hopscotch squares was in their hands. They laughed, skipped and ran for hours before Rebecca stuck her head out the front or back doors and called out, "Robert! Craig! Edwin! Ressey! Deborah! Faye! Portia!"

A second later, Rebecca gazed out the window, chuckled and mused to herself all the reasons Portia fit into her brothers' games with equal finesse that she mixed herself up in all the games her sisters chose to play. Rebecca couldn't help thinking that, in each of her pursuits, Portia was like a cornerstone. The way she coaxed her siblings and the neighborhood children to go along with her amusement ideas, the way she worked as a mediator and broke up fights, the way she made enemies shake hands, embrace and become friends, she seemed a born leader, a conqueror, a unique child.

It was Portia who stomped over to Denny late on Sunday evenings when the sun was tucking itself behind the trees in the back yard. She'd make her way across the living room like an Army drill sergeant displeased with a spot on a soldier's shirt. "Dad, you forgot to give us our lunch money for the coming week." She'd hold out her hand and tap her foot on the floor while she waited. Denny would laugh while he leaned back in his lounge chair and dug to the bottom of his pocket. Portia never asked for anything just for herself. Whenever she called out, "Mama! Dad!" and beckoned Denny or Rebecca to her side, she found ways to include her brothers and sisters in her requests.

Rebecca turned away from gazing out the window when the neighborhood children gathered their chants and raced around the building corner. Denny stood behind her. He smiled at her and cocked his head toward the kitchen archway. Rebecca turned and looked toward the archway. Her gaze fell across her own children's faces. Their legs and arms were coated with a powdery layer of dust.

She pursed her lips and shook her head while she slid her gaze down her children's arms and legs.

Breaking rank, Portia stepped to the front of her siblings, looked her mother squarely in the eye and pronounced, "We'll wash off before we eat, Mama. We were outside playing. We won't get the house dirty. Don't be mad at us. We had a lot of fun."

**Chapter 4**

### Wishes

Wishes floated up to Portia out of a well she thought empty. Wishes moved her stocking covered feet backwards. Wishes moved her outside Dennis' thick, warm arms. She longed to see his face . . . watch his thoughts reveal themselves in the arch of his brow . . . in the strength of his jaw. She wanted to see if he was afraid that, two years ago, he decided to love her. She wanted to see if his eyes would reveal to her whether or not he would love her tomorrow, next week, a month, a year from now. She stared at him bug-eyed. She thought she saw resolution that he would love her forever in his face. The thought took her again inside his embrace. He tightened his arms around her back and stroked her spine.

She ran the back of her hand across her face heavily. Snot spouted out of her nose and dribbled onto her mouth. Her voice quacked like a big, deep bucket banging the inside of an empty well. "How will I tell Mama . . . Dad?"

Like an echo making its way up through a deep valley, life gave her the answer. There were no other tests she could take. She'd reached the end of modern medicine. Pills wouldn't work. There was nothing she could swallow that would make her whole again. If she took a thousand shots a day, in the morning she'd still wake up with breast cancer. Her last visit to Dr. Kirnan's office was matter-of-fact. Despite her "I'm okay. I'm all right" claims, Dennis accompanied her.

"So, you're the lucky man," Dr. Kirnan said while he smiled at Dennis.

"Dennis nodded. "Yes." Then he turned and looked at Portia. "I certainly am."

"Portia." Dr. Kirnan leaned forward. He looked directly into her eyes. "You've been an excellent patient." Then he looked at Dennis and smiled again. "Ever since she was a little girl, she's been an excellent patient. Hardly ever sick. The few times she was, it was always something minor except for that one time she broke her arm. Her dad told me she was climbing a neighbor's apple tree. Wasn't supposed to be up there."

Portia lowered her head and grinned.

"Then there was that time she had meningitis. That wasn't a fun time, but she pulled through with flying colors. I don't think she cried once. Portia isn't one for complaining. And, you know," he faced her again. "You haven't changed. Not since you were a little girl coming in here with your mom and dad. Remember how you used to ask me for a grape lollipop before you left the office?"

She nodded.

He leaned back in his chair. "This isn't an easy time. I know that, but we're on our way to healing your body, and that's very good. Tomorrow you're gonna be on the mend, young lady. I'm going to go in and make an incision you won't even notice months from now. When I walk in that hospital tomorrow morning, you're going to be the only thing on my mind. I'm going to take good care of you. Of that, you can rest assured."

"I know Dr. Kirnan. I know you're going to take good care of me. When I told Mom and Dad I had breast cancer they asked me if you were treating me. When I told them that you were, you should have seen their shoulders lower. They were relieved at once to know you were seeing me through this."

"Good."

"What time do I have to be at the hospital again?"

"I'd like for you to be there by 8:00 tomorrow morning. It'll give me time to talk with you briefly and the nurses time to prep you for surgery." He looked at her. "Any other questions? You've got a funny expression on your face."

"I've probably asked you this before, but is it going to hurt?"

"You won't feel a thing. We're gonna put you to sleep."

"And I can go home tomorrow?"

He nodded. "And you can go home tomorrow."

"Is this going to cure her?"

Portia and Dr. Kirnan turned and looked at Dennis.

"I mean. After the surgery tomorrow, she's going to be okay?"

"Dennis—"

Dr. Kirnan raised his hand. "No. He should ask questions. She will be taking radiation treatments after tomorrow's lumpectomy."

"Then she'll be well?"

"She should be."   He looked from Dennis to Portia. "Anymore questions?"

"When can I go back to work?"

Dr. Kirnan chuckled.  "Such a worker you are.  You should be back to work in a week or so.  Let's wait and see how things go.  I expect the surgery to go well.  You should be back to work sooner than you think."

She stood.

"Is that all?"

"Yes."

"I should drive her directly to the hospital tomorrow?"

He nodded at Dennis.   "Yes.   Take her directly to the hospital.  I'll meet you there."

## Chapter 5

### Summer

Portia sat next to Dennis starting farewell letters then ripping them to shreds. "Dear Mama, I'm on my way home from the hospital. Last week, I spent two days finalizing my will. . . . Dear Dad, You know what I'm going to miss most about you? Your smile and the quiet way you make your presence known around the house. . . . Dear Edwin, I love you like you were my own. I don't know what it is about you, but of all of us, you're my favorite. . . . Dear Deborah, You can have my black pin stripped suit. You know. The one I wore to cuz's wedding. I've seen you eyeballing it. It's your's. . . . Dear Robert, Stay out of trouble with women. I always thought you worked too hard at being a player. . . . Dear Craig, If you ever get up the courage to let yourself really fall in love with a woman, make sure you love her for who she is on the inside. God knows. A woman never really knows what's going to happen to her body as time rolls along. . . . Dear Faye, I put my house in your name. It's paid for. If you decide to keep it, don't change a thing in my living room or the bedroom. Those are my two favorite rooms in the rancher. If you sell it, make sure you get a good price for it. I put a lot of work into that house the ten years I've owned it. . . . Dear Ressey, Keep your eye on Dennis for me. I don't want none of those conniving women getting their hands on him after I'm gone. . . ." Her bottom lip drooped, and she tossed the bits of scribbled on, torn paper across the floor of the car.

A second later, her mouth went into a crooked smile while she sat next to Dennis. He drove her home from her lumpectomy. Everyone from Dr. Kirnan to the nurses to the receptionist at the hospital's front desk doted on her before her lumpectomy. After the operation, quiet came around her. Except for Dr. Kirnan, the same people who smiled and told her, "It'll be all right," hung their heads and pretended not to see her while she walked by them feeling like less of a woman. Their discomfort flushed her thoughts with shame.

Like a thousand emergencies clamoring for her attention, she worried over the loss of Dennis, her family, her friends and her clients until she thought she heard sirens blare, whistle and scream inside her head. Life's crazy dance with death would take the people she loved and fought for most from her. Her faith in God and Jesus, the Christ, would still make room for a separation that could easily span a millennium. She told herself, after she made it to heaven, she'd still be waiting for their laughter, their soft smiles, their songs, their dance and their love to rejoin her -- to work like God made clay to make her whole again. "Oh, Dennis! Oh, Mama! Oh, Daddy!" she cried out. "I'm going to miss you. God knows I'm going to miss you! Oh, Dennis!" The nape of her neck pressed against the headrest. "I'm going to miss all of you. Everybody I love. All of you. All of you. Miss you. I will."

Dennis turned and stared at her. His jaw dropped, and his lip quivered. He hated to watch her grope for rescue from the pain breast cancer brought into her life. He felt helpless sitting next to her. He gawked at the open road. A nagging ache stabbed him in the heart each time he turned and looked at her with longing. He wished he had the power to speak peace to the great storm that raged in her life. He wished he could climb Jacob's ladder and knock on heaven's door. Knock on heaven's door and plead long and tirelessly with God to change the course of Portia's life -- beg God to make her well, separated from breast cancer and again vibrant, happy and strong. A second later, he took her hand inside his and squeezed it. He didn't let go of her hand until he looked up and saw her house. Turning on the blinkers, he pressed the accelerator, and his car bumped its way up the side drive.

Bowing her head and burying it inside her hands, Portia squeezed her temples. When she sat erect, her head was spinning. Her eyes ached from crying. She leaned back on the seat and eased the urgency of her thoughts into a week ago.

Though nothing soothed her like the warmth of her mother's love, she had to admit it was Denny's company she ached for soon after she discovered her left breast was diseased with cancer. Denny was easier to talk to, because he wasn't bull headed like she found her mother to be. He didn't argue for facts about breast cancer and survival statistics involving lumpectomies the way her mother did when she stood in the center of their living room and told them, "I have cancer. There's a tumor in my left breast. It's malignant."

A moment later, Dennis broke up her memory when he leaned toward her and said, "We're home." He gently rocked her shoulders. The pen she scribbled the shredded letters with rolled off her lap onto the floor. "Come on, Baby. We're home."

The morphine Dr. Kirnan prescribed for her as a painkiller made her reach out and search for Dennis. The drug-fog blurred her vision and seemed to move things away from her. Dennis held her hand while he guided her out of his car and closer -- closer to her house. Before they neared the front door, she lowered her head. Dennis' arm cradled her rocking hips while she walked next to him up her front porch steps.

In the house, she went immediately to the sofa. She refused to think about the operation while tears pooled in her eyes. She turned all her thoughts toward her family. The entire left side of her upper body was stiff. Her eyes kept opening and closing under the haze of morphine. She barely spoke to Dennis even though he talked to her non-stop while he went into the closet and pulled out a blanket. She kicked off her shoes and lay down. Her body was hot like she had a high fever. Nausea threatened to send her breakfast away from her stomach and again outside her mouth. Her mind reached for days when her body was strong and vibrant, to days when her parents pampered her when she had so much as a bad cold, to days when the hardest thing she had to think about was how to have fun during the summer.

Trouble couldn't take two weeks of vacation away from her family during the summer. Just thinking about it made her wish she was a little girl again. Rebecca always took them shopping for shorts and short sleeved shirts at the end of the school year. Denny always stuck his head under the hood of the family station wagon and changed the oil and belts the week of the Fourth of July. After firecrackers ripped through the sky and cousins, aunts, uncles and grandparents returned home from the barbecue they had in their back yard, the Fowler family climbed inside their station wagon and headed for the interstate.

For them, vacationing out of town during the summer was tradition. Only once did Boiling Automotive decline Denny's July 1-16 vacation request. Rebecca refused to travel out of town any other time. Teaching summer English courses, lecturing at community colleges, attending out-of-state education conferences and chairing writing seminars consumed all of her other summer break free time.

When Portia was a girl, her parents always took her brothers, sisters and her somewhere different to vacation. Sometimes the places -- the boardwalk at Atlantic City, their great-grandfather Fowler's house down South in Alabama, visiting historic black American sites -- ran together for her.

The summer her family went to Amusement World was the summer her father marched 150 South Side residents to the mayor's house. The weather was hot and sticky. Her father threatened to keep the family in Chicago that summer; it was so hot outside. Then he was hauled off to jail. The morning he came home from jail, all Portia heard him talking to her mother about was getting out of the city for a few days.

That summer vacation trek, Portia was shocked that her mama kept her hand tucked in her lap and away from seven year old Faye's mouth. "How far has Daddy gone?" Faye asked every five minutes. Rebecca counted mile markers and each time Faye asked how far they rode, she shouted out a number.

At each rest area their parents urged them to "at least try" to use the bathroom. Yet, ten year old, Craig, sat in the car. He never had to pee until Denny drove twenty miles passed the nearest rest area. While Craig squirmed, Portia stared at his wiggling knees.

Ressey and Deborah giggled most of the way to Florida. Robert and Edwin shifted in their seats a lot, and were taciturn most of the trip. For two days, Portia, not one for being still, sat in the back seat of the station wagon either asleep or furious.

Conditions worsened when they reached Amusement World. Portia, her sisters and brothers spent the day shouting, "There aren't enough rides! We thought there'd be rides all over the park! We rode only three rides all day! You have us in the wrong side of the park! We don't have enough money to have any fun! We can't even get on rides!"

Because they needed to laugh and cast their cares to the wind, Rebecca and Denny adored Amusement World. They held hands while they walked in and out of souvenir shops. They stood in long lines to board slow rides. They sat beneath umbrella covered tables and nibbled chili dogs and sipped orange juice.

The morning after they visited Amusement World, Denny checked his family out of their three hotel rooms and drove twenty miles North of the hotel to a beach. That day, Rebecca and he watched their children run up and down the sandy shore.

'Colored Only' signs hammered into the ground across the street from the hotel they stayed in, the day at the beach gave the Fowler family a strong sense of freedom. A light wind pushed at their backs; a gentle sun warmed their heads. While Rebecca and Denny watched Portia and her siblings run, they wondered what the future would push inside their lives.

# Chapter 6

## *Mama*

Portia folded her arms across her stomach and sighed. It had been three weeks since her lumpectomy and one week since she was first treated with the cobalt machine. When Dennis was unable to free himself from the university, Deborah drove her to and from her radiation treatments.

"Why won't you take chemotherapy? I thought you said Dr. Kirnan told you chemo and radiation are better than only radiation treatments?"

Portia pursed her lips while she stared at the side of her oldest sister's head. "Because I don't want to go bald."

Deborah chuckled while she drove away from the cancer care center. "Oh, Portia. You've never been vain. You've always been more of a spiritual woman." She chuckled again. "And when you weren't in the Spirit, you were too busy being a tomboy to care two cents what you looked like."

Portia laughed outright. "Just because I love God, doesn't mean I want to lose all my hair. Besides, I've always been one to say God only knows how much money pharmaceutical companies make off of this stuff they pump into our bodies. Sometimes I wonder if medical scientists really care what all these drugs do to our bodies and how tired and sick they make us feel. Sometimes I wonder if money's not the name of the game. I know I shouldn't say that, but that's how I feel sometimes." She peered down at her hands. "Sometimes I do. Since I started my treatments, my skin's started itching, and the horror stories I've heard about the burns you get from the radiation. Goodness. And, Girl, a lady at the center was taking chemo for six months. She said those six months a few strands of hair came out here and there, but she thought she was home free as far as hair loss goes. Then, at the end of those six months, she lost all of her hair in one day!"

Deborah's eyes swelled. "What?"

Portia nodded "Yeah. 24-hours." She ran her hand across the top of her head. "Gone! Every strand. And not only head hair. Child, you lose your eyebrows, your eyelashes -- all-of-your-hair.

Can you imagine what it would be like to have to deal with that on top of the treatments and the operations? Goodness."

"Ump!"

"Plus, I didn't have any positive lymph nodes. My cancer was localized, so Dr. Kirnan didn't push for me to accept chemo."

"Dr. Kirnan's good people. He's always gone away from mainstream."

Portia laughed. "I know. That white man has always treated us like we were family -- as chocolate as we are."

A gust of wind badgered the car's windows while Deborah drove around a corner and down a stretch of road lined with fast food restaurants. A popular jazz cut was playing on the radio. Portia and Deborah silenced the music; they laughed so loud.

"Dr. Kirnan is good people. I just wish he'd put you in another center. I don't like that nurse who's always there. She's too matter-of-fact about you having breast cancer if you ask me. She's always telling you to raise your left arm above your head. She's always telling you to--" Twisting her lips, Deborah raised her voice and talked in a squeaky monotone. 'Relax. Relax. Take it easy, Honey. Millions of women have been through this. Relax. Just relax.'"

"You can tell she hasn't been through it personally. Had her body cut on like that."

"She makes as much sense as a nurse who's never been pregnant telling a woman in labor to stop sweating, crying and screaming."

"Girl. Don't talk about having kids. Just thinking about it, makes me want to grab my stomach and rock from side to side."

They laughed.

"Portia, you always were crazy. You always knew how to make me laugh. Remember that time Chucky tried to get with you?"

"Deborah, don't start. Please don't start."

"What grade were you in?"

"Deborah."

"The ninth grade?"

Portia pursed her lips. "Something like that. I was young."

"And such a tomboy. You didn't have no time for boys. You were sports all the way."

"Doctors say being athletic will decrease a woman's risk for getting breast cancer."

"Portia."

"No. They do. I've read that in I don't know how many books."

"Well. Nothing works all the time. I don't care what you're talking about, what the subject is. Nothing works all the time."

She twisted her mouth. "I guess not. I'm living proof of that. For sure I am."

"Just keep your faith in God. You're on the right track. You're whole on the inside. Your body can't help but to catch up with all the good things that are going on inside of your heart, inside your spirit."

"Thanks, Sis."

Deborah pointed, "Girl, look!"

"If that dude ain't looking like Darryl."

Portia leaned forward on the passenger seat. "Girl, that is Darryl!"

"Looking drunker than ten boy sailors." She winked at Portia. "Here. Want me to pull over so you can ask him back, tell him how you can't live without him."

Extending her leg, Portia placed her foot over the top of Deborah's and pressed down on the accelerator. "Girl, you better gas this car."

Both sisters laughed until they neared a crosswalk. "Look at her," Deborah said pointing to a woman in a halter.

Portia rolled her eyes.

"She knows she's too big to wear that halter."

Without taking her eyes off the woman's heavy, bouncing breasts, Portia pulled on her windbreaker until it covered her own left breast.

Deborah and Portia talked about the nurse at the cancer care center, Portia's oncologist, her radiologist, Dr. Kirnan, heavy-busted women, men and work until they reached Portia's ranch house. Deborah stayed at Portia's house eating tangelos and sipping lemonade until the grandfather clock bonged.

Turning in her chair, Deborah looked up and saw that it was two o'clock. "Gotta go, Girl. I have to pick that crazy boyfriend of mine up from his part-time job. He's working a part-time and a full-time job now."

"Wwhhaatt?"

Deborah stood. "You heard me right. You finished with your glass?"

"Yeah. Why? You trying to be helpful?"

Deborah laughed while she walked into the kitchen and sat the two glasses in the sink. After she returned to the room, she leaned against the arch in the front doorway. "Yes. I'm being helpful. And why not? Can't I be, Miss-do-everything-for-herself? Miss-don't-ever-want-anybody-to-help-her?"

Portia waved her hand. "Oh, shut up. And I ain't getting up either."

Deborah laughed. "Why should you? You never do?"

"So, Xavier's working two jobs now?"

Deborah turned and faced the storm door. "Stop, Portia. Don't you even get started talking down on Xavier. You lucked up with Dennis, Girl. You know God was smiling on you when he gave you that good man."

"I'm just surprised that Xavier's working at all." Portia leaned forward on the sofa. She wore a crooked grin. "You know, as in working period?"

"Let me go."

"That's right. Hurry and grab your keys and get on out of here before I get on you about the men you date."

"Oh, shut up, Portia. You've got a good man. I'm still trying to land me a decent man. After those last three months Xavier was out of work, I laid down the law about him carrying his load."

"I'm sure you did."

"Girl."

"No. I'm serious. I believe you."

"Then why are you smirking?"

"No reason."

"Um-hmmmm. Shoot. Girl. The kind of men I keep bumping into. If I were in your shoes, Xavier would have left me six months before I found out I had breast cancer if he even sensed something hard was coming down the pike. I'd have had to catch the bus home from my lumpectomy."

Lifting a pillow off the sofa, Portia threw it at Deborah. "Get out of here!"

With a smile on her face, Deborah hurried across the floor and hugged Portia. She rubbed Portia's back while she told her, "Later, Girl. I love you. Take it easy." A moment later, Portia was alone.

The silence in the house built and lengthened until it became like a loud noise. Yet, instead of turning on the television or the radio, Portia told herself, besides the nurse at the cancer care center, she hated the way the oncologist dotted the area of her breast surrounding her lumpectomy. She hated those tumor markers. She hated the times the hospital staff drew her blood. She hated feeling like she had the flu every day. Despite the fatigue, not once did she take a sick day from work. She fought and won three of her last four cases. She only allowed her fatigue to reveal itself when she was alone at home.

Deborah outside her company, she stretched out on the sofa. When her head went against one of the sofa's pillows, her thoughts went to the woman who taught her how to fight, fight hard, reach down into the pit of her gut for her deepest strength, and, from that point, jab her life's hardest troubles with her faith in God -- with the love her people sent into her life.

Her mama.

None of the women in her mama's family were passive. Like the gone to the earth matriarchs in her family, Portia knew Rebecca learned to reach her dreams by way of fight. Words were her weapons, and, astute with American English, words served her well. Portia knew Rebecca was proud of their culture. Under no circumstances did she tolerate racial bashing. Injustice, she execrated. When Portia looked back, she realized that the price for her mama's mental attitude was cruel . . cruel like cancer had come into her breast and turned her life into a cruel, vicious dance with death. Closing her eyes and nodding into a stupor filled with thoughts about yesteryear, Portia pushed her shoulders against the sofa. A faint smile tugged at the corners of her mouth. She was proud of her mother for enduring America's hard, hidden racism of the 1970's.

Coworkers abandoned Rebecca when she went against Dr. Harold Davidson, Director of the State Department of Education. Despite the director's request, during the spring of 1972, she refused to read Racial Heritage, a novel that showed Southern whites as creators and innovative thinkers and Southern blacks as slothful servants possessing marginal intelligence. "Due to the fact that hypocrisy, racism and segregation have no place in American society, I fail to see why Racial Heritage should be *required* reading in our state's public high school English courses," she wrote in her April 27, 1972 letter to the director. Next, she suggested Maya Angelou and her work, I Know Why The Caged Bird Sings. Her argument became, "After all, that's the text the state colleges are reading this summer in preparation for Welcome Week." Adding pulse to the sting, she voiced her opinion unreservedly in all of her classes. Looking back to that spring, Portia found her mama to be unusually moody. Brushing her shoulder as they trudged up and down their home's carpeted living room stairwell, she feared her resignation or worse, Dr. Davidson's request for it.

*August 29, 1972*

*Dear Mama,*

*How are Dad and you? I'm fine. Enjoying the apartment, though I can do without the bills. High school'll be starting again soon. Excited? Not ready? Anxious? It won't be long. How's Edwin? Is he walking in circles and stomping around the house yet? Labor Day looms. Don't worry. Soon he'll be graduated and enrolled in some prestigious institution of higher education.*

*They have a part-time job here, but I don't want to tell Edwin about it. Never mind Dad and you drumming into our heads that work is work and any work is good so long as it's honest. I don't want my brother being any lawyer's janitor. He can do much better than that. I ran into Deborah and Faye the other day at the grocery store. We were all broke so we chipped our money together and bought candy! Sound nutritious?*

*Well, I'm gonna run.*

*Take care.*

*Love you both!*

## Portia

Portia rolled to her side. Her back and shoulders swayed while she leaned across the edge of the sofa until she had what she wanted in her hands -- a 600-page medical text. Strength escaped her body when she gave a long, deep breath to the room. Dismissing the weak spell with the iron in her will, she told herself she wasn't feeble. She told herself her body was reacting to what she'd been reading day and night for the past four weeks.

Breast cancer was the focus of her life. She read about it on her way to work. She read about it at newsstands and in bookstores and at the library. She telephoned Dr. Kirnan several times a week and badgered his patience with questions she didn't resolve through the readings. The more she discovered about the disease, the less trapped she felt. It was an uncanny dilemma. Her obsession, though in many ways disengaging her from fear, kept cancer with her mind, with her spirit -- even in her sleep. She wondered if the food she ate would feed the tumor and cause it to grow. She stared at the paint on her house walls; in the office she wondered if there could be asbestos. Yet, she kept telling herself her pain would pass. . . . One day she wouldn't have to cry herself to sleep. She'd stop dreaming about days gone by spent with family. She'd stop looking into the toilet each time she urinated, checking to see if she'd dropped blood, as if the cancer moved from her left breast to her bladder in a matter of weeks.

There was an air of sorrow about Portia as she stretched out on the sofa. The medical text was closed and laying flat against her stomach. Reading the old letter she never mailed, because she spent the first month after she wrote it claiming she was too busy at Courtney & Sons to go to the post office, didn't shake her pain. Inside her head, ideas bounced against one another then separated like popcorn. She felt crazed with pain. Thoughts of yesterday kept surfacing. Reading the thirteen-year-old letter, its edges torn and faded, deepened her nostalgia. After tucking it inside the medical text, she sat up and stared at the wall across from the sofa. When she lay down again, her mind rested on her mama.

Born and raised in Alabama, Rebecca Armstrong grew up searching for an exit, a way out of the ghetto. Each time she looked, the door out was the same – education. When she finished rolling tobacco and picking cotton alongside her grandmother, she hurried through dinner. Her plate washed and dried and back on the shelf, her feet couldn't hurry to the back of the house fast enough. If she got there before Old Tilley, the family cat, went hunting after rats in the alley, she could read for an hour before her grandmother came to bed.

"Turn that light out!" That was the first thing her grandmother would holler at her if she wasn't laying flat on her back in the dark by the time she came scooting inside their small room.

"More like a closet," her grandmother would say, a chuckle rumbling in her throat. "More like a closet," she'd say when Rebecca's friends would visit and ask Rebecca if she had her own room.

"Not like a closet, not really," Rebecca would think to herself while her grandmother cackled in front of her friends. "Two closets put together maybe, but not just one."

What Rebecca longed to show her friends in her bedroom was the books. Walls of books. Books climbing up the walls like crazy vine. But her grandmother told her when she was real young, "Ain't no comp'ny 'llowed back here. Don't you go bringin' yo frien's back here. Be a lady. Yo bedroom is a privat'cy place."

When she entered high school she told herself to read a book a day, five days a week. Birthday and holiday money went to buy books. It wasn't until her grandmother scooted into the bedroom half an hour earlier than usual and asked her, "Why you always readin? Why you read so much?" that she started to think about what she wanted to do with her life.

That night she raised her shoulders and said, "Um-um."

Her grandmother sat on the edge of the bed and pulled her shoes off with an "unh". Her shoes off, she pulled on her long nightgown. "Don't know?"

Rebecca raised her shoulders again. "Not sure."

"How ol' you, gurl?"

"Fifteen."

"I was married wit' three chil'rens by da time I was your age. What 'chu mean you don't know what you want to do wit' your life?

What kinda answer is that comin' from a gurl who be readin' all da time?"

Rebecca raised her shoulders again. "Um-um."

"That all you can say?"

"No, Ma'am."

"Give me an answer, gurl!"

"I don't know, Grandma."

"You ain't goin' to bed 'til you give me an answer. You hear me right here and right now!"

"Yes, Ma'am."

"Answer me, gurl!"

"I wanna be somebody."

"You can talk better'n that. Just 'cause I ain't learned, don't mean you gotta be stupid."

"You ain't stupid, Grandma."

"I know that, but I ain't got all that book sense you got. You make me proud. The way you be readin' an' all. Make me stay out front longer just so you can read in here all by yo'self. Think I don't be doin' it on purpose."

"Grandma."

"You goin' do somethin' with yo'self, gurl. I ain't goin' have it no other way. You hear me, gurl!"

"Yes. Ma'am." She closed her book and turned out the light.

A second later, the light was on again. "What 'chu doin'?"

"Going to bed, Grandma. I'm getting ready to say my prayers. I'm not going to go to bed without saying my prayers." She waited. "You want to say your prayers with me, Grandma." She waited another minute. "You want you and me to say our prayers together tonight, Grandma."

"We can do that, but that ain't what I turned that light back on fo' and you knows that. Don't play possum wit' me, gurl."

"I want—I – I – I want to be a – I want to teach kids how to read and write. I – I – I want to be a teacher."

Her grandmother banged her hand against the night table. "Say it plain! Say it plain, gurl! Mean eve'y word of it!"

Rebecca straightened her spine. "I want to be a teacher."

It took ten years of reading, writing and studying. Rebecca didn't give up. Each time she felt like giving up, she heard her grandmother shouting, "Say it plain, gurl! Mean eve'y word of it!" Portia was fifteen herself before Rebecca became secure as a teacher. Students challenged her, but they didn't plant fear in her. Teenagers the school board said belonged in prison came into her class sleeping and nodding. By the end of the year they were passing with ease and leading group discussions. Regardless of what the school board said about Jefferson, Rebecca filled with hope when she looked out at the students in her class. She wouldn't teach anywhere else.

Located at 390 South Chicago Avenue, half an acre of woodland spread across the back of Jefferson High School. In the spring, blossoming flowers gave the school a stately appearance.

Regularly city newspapers, and, no less than a dozen times, the state's major newspaper, immortalized accomplishments made by Jefferson's students. The trenchant newspaper articles made Chicago's entire black community proud.

Tyson and Rodgers, Chicago's two other predominantly black high schools, produced the city's finest athletic squads. Jefferson won only two state crowns in athletics since its inception in 1911, and those were in basketball. More popular subjects at Jefferson were Science, Theatre and English.

Jerome Morgan was the first man to discover blood plasma that helped control sickle cell anemia. Milton Davis, Priscilla Werne, Timothy Jones and Tiffany Howard were members of The Company of Playhouse H. Reneae Howard and Carlton Dever traveled across America in a musical comedy. Gary Stuart was a community activist and a United States representative at the United Nations. Tony Wright, LeSalle Turner, Philip Bezak and Donald Hawthorne were published poets and novelists. All were Jefferson graduates.

Jefferson's principal was a short, stout, heavy-footed woman named Sheila Williams. Jefferson's vice-principal was a soft spoken, tall, stocky man named Darryl White. Together they knew two hundred students, Jefferson's average graduating class, was large enough a number to change discrimination laws and questionable corporate ethics . . . if not halt them. They realized that forty years into the future, Jefferson's Class of 1972 would be a neighborhood . .

. several communities . . . a small town. It was, therefore, that they demanded nothing less than one hundred percent from their faculty.
\*\*\*\*\*\*\*\*\*\*\*\*\*\*\*\*\*\*\*\*\*\*\*\*\*\*\*\*\*\*\*\*\*\*\*\*\*\*\*\*\*\*\*\*\*\*\*\*\*\*\*\*\*\*\*\*\*\*\*\*\*\*\*

Rebecca stood with her feet spread apart. She inhaled deeply before she spoke. "A Civil Rights Act was passed by Congress in 1964. Title VI of that Civil Rights Act prohibits discrimination in federally assisted programs. Section 601 of Title VI of the Civil Rights Act prohibits discrimination by any organization based on race, color, or national origin receiving financial assistance from the federal . . ."

She hushed before she offered, "Good afternoon, Students. Be attentive." She raised her right index finger. "Examine the language. During today's class I hope to persuade you to believe that we are accountable for the things we say, the things we use English to convey or express. The Civil Rights Act of 1964 tells us that we can be punished for discriminating, and, of course, discrimination can be verbal." She walked around her desk and stood in the center of the room. "I read those sections of Title VI of the Civil Rights Act to you because I know it's unlikely that you will read them yourselves. You trust your congressmen and congresswomen." She grinned. "It's imperative that you familiarize yourselves with a few of our country's laws. But that's not what I'm driving at. To iterate, during today's class, I'm going to illustrate the power of words. How we say or write things and when we say or write things is crucial. English is important. So often language is the vital organ in our triumphs." She strolled back to her desk and stood behind it. "I hope I've impressed the attorney in each of you. I know you're anxious to present your summaries on Richard Wright's <u>Native Son.</u>" She chuckled. "After teaching English for twenty-seven years, I know how eager students are to stand before their classmates and speak." She grinned shamelessly. "I'm ready to listen to your summaries. I know each of you is well prepared." She rounded the corner of her desk and walked to the center of the room. At the room's center, she stilled her feet. "Calvin!"

Calvin jumped.
"Dana!"
Dana held her breath.
"Lisa!"

Lisa froze.

"One of you. Somebody." She waited. "Somebody, anybody, get up. I want to hear a summary." She paced the front of the room. "David."

David wore an I-don't-believe-Mrs.Fowler-called-on-me expression.

She nodded at David's glare. "Yes, Sir. You. Yes, David. I called on you."

David muttered, "Ahhh."

She peered at him. "David, before this school year is over, you and every student in this classroom will learn to be confident. You will stop cowering when I call upon you to speak before your classmates, because you will have a firm grasp of the English language. I know this is the second week of the school year, but as I said last week, my classes consists of fifty percent reading, twenty-five percent writing and twenty-five percent public speaking. So, David, stand up and read me your summary."

David's eyes were downcast. When he stood, he held, between quivering fingers, the three sheets of ruled notebook paper his summary was written on. "Native Son, authored by Richard Wright . . ."

David's summary finished, Rebecca stepped close to him and smiled. "You wrote an excellent summary."

David nodded and grinned sheepishly. "Thank you."

"Certainly." Rebecca turned and faced the center of the class. "Tammy." She paused. "Caroline, Patricia, Alex, Reggie, one of you five students read your classmates and me your summary."

At the end of forty-five minutes, fourteen of Rebecca's twenty-eight, third period English students read their book summary. Rebecca stood in the center of the room. "Students, you all did well. I was impressed. Your summaries were well written, incisive. Good. Now, I want to combine them with the Civil Rights Act of 1964." She took in a deep breath. "I want none of you to tolerate discrimination. Color is irrelevant; don't tolerate discrimination. I also hope for none of you to be ignorant. Ignorance is a vicious trap. Ignorance leads to weakness and death. Read often. Open your minds, and flood them with good things. When you write, attempt to write well. And when you can, help someone else become more learned, to become stronger. Wisdom, love, and an unbreakable inner strength, with God's grace, will help you prosper in this world."

## Chapter 7

### *Grandparents*

Nausea from the sixth week of radiation treatments curdled in Portia's stomach, made its way up her throat, then to the corners of her graying mouth. She sat on the edge of her sofa, placed her head in the palm of her hand, and closed her eyes. Her head started to bob and weave, so she lay on the sofa again. She slept for two hours. When she awoke, Dennis was standing over her.

"Wake up. Come on, Baby. Wake up."

Portia heard a woman scream when she bolted into a sitting position.

Dennis sat next to her and wrapped his arms around her shoulders. "Ssshhh," he whispered to her while he pecked her forehead and the sides of her face. "You must have had a bad dream. When I walked through the front door, you were screaming."

Portia wiped sweat from her forehead, then leaned her head against Dennis' shoulder. "I was at The Chronicle's Christmas party." Her shoulders trembled. She clutched Dennis' waist. "I was the only one at the party who didn't have any clothes on. I had these two big, gaping holes in my chests -- where my breasts used to be."

"Baby, you still have your breasts."

Her voice rocked. Words came out of her mouth as if they had a jagged edge. "I know. I know. But, everybody was staring at me." Tears inched down her face until her cheeks grew hot. She buried the side of her face behind Dennis' shoulder. "Everybody was staring at me, and I couldn't get out of the room. I co-cou-I couldn't find the door. I couldn't get out."

"You're not at The Chronicle's party, Baby. You're here with me." He kissed her forehead. "You're right here with me."

Her shoulders heaved. "I'll never be the same, Dennis."

"No. You'll be better. You're stronger. You're more in tune with your feelings, with who you really are."

"Having cancer isn't a bonus, Honey."

"I know that. I wasn't saying that. It's just that you're looking at who you really are more. You're a beautiful, intelligent, loving, warm, thoughtful, caring woman. You're somebody very, very special, Portia."

She wept.

Dennis sat on the sofa with her for fifteen minutes holding and rocking her. "Feel better?"

She nodded.

"You look sleepy."

"I'm always sleepy anymore."

"You're doing good, Baby. You really are. I don't know if I could handle the situation as well as you are if the tables were reversed. I mean. You haven't missed a day from work since you recovered from your operation. You keep your house up. And you look like a zillion bucks." He stood from the sofa, leaned and kissed her forehead.

"Gotta get back to work?"

"Yeah. I wanted to stop by during my break. I'm giving my early evening class a test today."

"All right." She extended her hand, and he let her fingers slide between his fingers. He kissed her on the mouth before he stepped away from her and said, "I better get back to the university. I'll call you before I'm finished with the test. When I call, let me know if you want me to pick you up anything special for dinner. If not, I'll just throw something together for dinner for us when I get back. And, oh," he called to her over his shoulder, "I'll pick up a jar of that aloe cream you told me Dr. Kirnan said you could use to help ease those radiation burns."

"Thanks. Bye, Baby." Those were the last words Portia said before she sunk back down onto the sofa and drifted off to sleep. An hour later, when she opened her eyes again, the fear of dying attacked her thoughts.

As a young girl playing in her grandparents' back yard, not for a second did she think she'd die – ever. As a teenager sitting in her grandparents' living room on Christmas Eve, music playing on the stereo, good food lining the dining room table – though she never voiced it, when she looked at her grandparents, she told herself, "I'll miss them when they're gone. It'll be so hard for me when they die."

She almost chuckled.

She was as close to her grandparents as Rebecca told her she was to her gone-to-the-earth grandmother. Birthdays weren't complete unless she stopped by her grandparents', not for a gift, just to see them. Talk with them. Laugh with them. She watched the way their hands moved. Listened to their Southern accent, still strong even after living in Chicago for more than twenty years. Sundays after church held special memories for her because that was the day she went walking with her grandmother, Katrina. "It'll help to keep her young and fit, make her live longer," she mused to herself while she smiled up at Katrina. Family reunions and Thanksgiving Dinner saw family traveling to Chicago from all parts of the country. It was nothing for 200 relatives to show up at a family reunion. Katrina or Priscilla's house was always crowded and loud on Thanksgiving Day.

Rolling to her side, Portia closed her eyes. A second later she opened them again. She fought off sleep. The sweetest memories hovered around her. Her shoulders heaved. "Trust God. It's gonna be all right," she whispered to the empty room. A moment later when her eyes closed, she drifted into a light sleep. It wasn't long before she heard her grandparents, Eddie and Katrina.

It was late September 1977. After a long, hot summer, temperatures dipped below the mid-70s. Leaves dried and faded from green to yellow, red, orange and brown. Winter lurched in the same wind that blew leaves off the sycamore tree standing proud and tall, its branches wide and claw-like, in the center of Eddie and Katrina's front yard.

Eddie rubbed his hands together and gazed out the living room window. All his eyes saw was the sycamore tree, growing more naked every day. His mind saw the first days of his four-year retirement. He chuckled while he thought about the many times his wife, Katrina, their children and grandchildren whispered, "Pops is gonna get bored. He's not going to know what to do with himself after not working just one month."

"Whew, Lord!" Eddie said before he laughed outright. "After working at Boiling Automotive for thirty-three years, I was more than ready to retire." He leaned back in his favorite lounge chair and told himself after Katrina and he ate dessert, he'd pull the blanket Portia crocheted for him twelve years ago out of the closet and take a short nap.

He crossed his legs at the ankles. A smile widened his face. He pulled a paperback novel close to his chest. "Awww, Ralph, talk to me," he offered with a shake of his head. Two hours passed before he placed the paperback on the coffee table and sighed.

Outside it was dusk. Grandchildren of the mostly over-fifty-years-old avenue residents tore up and down the sidewalks engaging in street races and games of freeze tag. The running children's grandparents sat on their front porches watching cars and their own grandchildren zip back and forth in front of them. Lightning bugs flickered and glowed. Mosquitoes zoomed in on the children and their grandparents and bit any leg or arm that dared not move. The day's heat was gone over the backs of the neighborhood houses with the sun. If Eddie turned in the lounge chair and looked out the picture window Katrina decorated with African and Indian figurines, he could watch it all happen.

Foregoing the neighborhood watch, he placed his thoughts on his wife of thirty-eight years and called over his shoulder, "Katrina!"

Standing over the stove stirring butterscotch pudding that was thickening fast, Katrina chuckled. It was Saturday night. For the last ten years, she made either sugar cookies or butterscotch pudding on Saturday night after Eddie cleared the dinner table and she washed and dried the dishes. They depended on the habits their combined lives took on. She almost stuck her finger inside the pan of hot pudding, the butterscotch smelled so good. "I'm in the kitchen making pudding."

"Like butterscotch pudding, don't you?"

She checked over the highest point of her shoulder to make certain he wasn't standing to the right of her in the dining room. She wore a sly grin. "Um-hmmm!" She watched the pudding thicken while it made bubbling sounds.

"I know that's right." While he called out to her, Eddie listened to Jamie and Reginald Baxter gently admonish their granddaughter, Montifah, to move closer to the edge of their front yard. After he heard the Baxters call Montifah a fourth time, he pushed himself from the chair.

He scooted his house shoe clad feet across the living room floor, through the dining room and into the kitchen. He stood behind Katrina and wrapped his thick arms around her waist, a waist that had expanded over the years but was still just right for him. "Butterscotch." He smiled and pecked her cheeks, the backs of her ears, her forehead, then her chin. "Mmmmm. Butterscotch is sweet."

Katrina chuckled. "Ummm-hmmm. Yes."

Eddie tightened his grip around her waist, and, pulling his chest against her back, he created a warm spot in the center of her spine. "And so are you."

Turning the fire beneath the stove out, she wiggled free of his embrace and lifted the pan of pudding off the front eye and placed it on a back burner. "Who're you telling?"

He turned and searched the cabinets for a bowl large enough to contain the pudding.

She watched his gaze move through the cabinets. "How's the book Portia bought you?" Her voice softened. "That child knows what you like. Ump! That girl is always getting somebody something. Rebecca said that child went and bought -- went right out and bought -- Denny and her a collection of Frederick Douglass' writings last month. Said something about she didn't think they were reading enough." She laughed. "Get that. Not reading enough." She chuckled. "Rebecca's been reading three books a week and teaching English for over twenty years." She smiled and shook her head. "Not reading enough."

Eddie stepped away from the cabinet closest to the refrigerator. He held a large glass, mixing bowl. His brow was arched. "But don't try to get her anything. Remember when we tried to get her that home movie camera -- her and her family root keeping self."

Katrina took the bowl into her hands. "Lord. That girl wouldn't have it. Said it cost too much money and that she was too old for us to be buying her stuff."

"Ain't she something?"

"I like that drive of hers, but she needs to learn how to let somebody do something nice for her every now and again." She shook her head. "I really don't know where that girl gets all that independence from. It's like she thinks it's a sin to ask for help."

"You can't say too much, Katrina."

"I ain't that independent. Not like Portia. Un-un."

"Naw. That's true. Wonder if it comes from growing up in such a big family."

"Why aren't any of Denny and Rebecca's other children like that then? Why aren't we like that, all those brothers and sisters we have?"

"Um-um. Guess it's just the way Portia is. You know." He gazed across the room. "I always thought there was something about that girl. Something special. I never said nothing about it, because I didn't want to make it seem like I thought more of her than I do our other grandchildren, because I don't. I love them all. Equal. But it's something about that Portia. Can't put my finger on it, but it's something."

"I know what it is." She smiled. "Insight. That girl has insight. It's like she can see into the future. Portia ain't no normal child, Ed. Now don't you go telling Rebecca or Denny I said this, but Rebecca told me for herself that Portia told her things about people in our family and people in their neighborhood long before it happened."

"Predicting the future?"

She nodded. "Rebecca said it herself."

He arched his brow. "Like what?"

"Like that time Ms. Baxter got that stroke. Rebecca said Portia kept pulling on her each time they saw Ms. Baxter. Kept telling Rebecca she was having dreams about Ms. Baxter. Said in the dreams Ms. Baxter's face was twisted, kept being twisted."

"What?"

"And Tim. You know Tim."

"Tim Carter?'

"Yeah. Him."

"So?"

"Rebecca said Portia saw Tim falling out of that truck of his six months before he got in that accident. Saw him falling down a hill the way he fell out of his truck and went rolling down that hill when that car hit him."

He was silent.

"And little Gloria."

"That little girl that died when Portia was in the third grade?"

"Rebecca said Portia was dreaming about her before she died too."

He turned in his chair until he faced Katrina. "Now, you're not saying Portia knows when people are gonna die, are you?"

She raised then lowered her shoulders. "Um-um. Just telling you what Rebecca told me. Something about that girl. Sure nuff."

He thought about what she said for a minute. A second later he decided he wanted to change the subject. He didn't tell Katrina, but he worried about Portia. He thought her seriousness, her deep thoughts were going to take a lot of life from her. When Katrina resumed stirring the pudding, he slapped his knee and bellowed, "Lord, yes. And the book -- ump! You know ol' Ralph. His latest mystery is good as usual." His mouth worked itself into a smile. "That Portia." He shook his head. "She sure doesn't mind spoiling her Pops."

Katrina neared the stove and the pot of pudding. "I knew you'd get into that book. When Portia brought it over here yesterday, I told her, Girl, Pops is gonna finish that book before church on Sunday."

Eddie walked to the kitchen table. He carried a tall glass of apple juice. "Yeah. Rebecca said Portia's coming along well at Courtney & Sons. I knew once she got her foot in the door, she'd take off. That girl really has a good head on her shoulders."

Katrina stuck her finger in the pudding. "Um-hmmm."

Eddie shook his head at the cold, smooth taste of the apple juice.

Sticking her finger into her jaw, Katrina pulled on her finger until all the butterscotch went inside her mouth. "I just hope she takes time out for herself. You know. Not become all work and no play. I worry about that child sometimes. She's so serious."

No longer thirsty, Eddie turned and smiled at Katrina's back. "Need any help?"

"No. When I get through scooping the pudding into the bowl you gave me, I'll sit it on the table right in front of you."

A minute later, steam pushed its way off the top of the pudding,. Butterscotch aroma escaped across the table. "Just for you, my sweet black man."

He leaned back in his chair. He watched her move toward the refrigerator. "Yeah, Ralph wrote another good one. I know I keep saying it, but I think Ralph's one of the best mystery writers of this century. He's got this guy, Claude Gordon, a Brother from the South Side, who won't go away." He chuckled. "I can't tell you what all Claude's been through. Everybody from Claude's ex-wife to Claude's banker to Claude's housekeeper -- can you believe this man lives in a two-bedroom house and has a house keeper? Anyhow, everybody's tried to knock the Brother off, but he keeps coming back. This book is wild. Claude's always getting in tight spots. It's been going pretty smooth lately. Claude's met this nice looking woman in her late 40s, and things are going pretty good for them so far . . . so far." He stopped and laughed.

She carried a glass of milk and two yellow bowls to the table. "So, tell me more about this mystery novel Ms. Portia brought over here just yesterday."
*****************************************************

Rain splashed against the windowpane. The wet pitter-patter plucked Portia off the sofa. Her eyes were tinted with yellow. She walked to the bureau. All she thought about was searching for a family picture, something she could tuck inside her memory, something she could use to make herself strong when she felt like dissecting her life into chunks of pain -- when she felt like falling apart.

When she reached the bureau, she grew light-headed and fell. Her knees banged onto the floor. Sweat popped out on her brow before she pulled her legs beneath her buttocks and sat. She started digging, her long, skinny fingers crawling over loose pieces of silverware, three high school year books and old letters sent to her from out-of-town friends. She dug through two legal note pads scribbled with names, addresses, dates, and police identification numbers, thin-necked wine glasses, and Christmas wrapping so old and dismissed, its print was faded. She opened and crawled her way through all six of the bureau's side drawers until she found the picture. She smiled at the faces in the photograph. She thought her grandmama and her mama, with a hint of red in the tips of their hair, looked rather satisfied with themselves in 1975.

The picture brought to Portia's memory the words a student of her mother's shared with her one hot summer day nearly twenty years ago. The words belonged to her mother. The student gawked at Portia and told her, "Your mama's always standing in front of us talking like she's an old sage or something. She's always telling us things her own mama told her when she was a little girl." The student chuckled. The sun hit her braces, and made them look like rows of polished silver in her mouth. "Your mom's always telling us," tossing her head back, the student narrowed her brow and heightened her shoulders. "Your mom's always saying, "'Regardless of the struggles you face, like our faith-filled, martyred, tireless ancestors, meet your challenges head on.'" Her brow tightened. "'Not one of you should ever give up on life. Not one of you should quit.'"

Pulling the family picture close to her breasts, Portia kissed the spot on the picture where her grandmother's and her mother's faces were.

## Chapter 8
### *Thanksgiving Day*

Portia stood, and crossed the floor. Her feet created whispers of ssshhh-ssshhh-sssshhhh while she scooted into the living room. To maintain her balance, she ran her hand along the wall. She stopped moving her feet when she reached the picture window. The drapes were closed.

She chuckled when she peered through the opening at the side of the drapes. The changing weather made her think about her Great-Grandma Armstrong. She imagined her voice cracking out, "Gul, I sho' gets ti'ed sometimes. That Alabama heat smack down on my neck, all 'round my black neck, and make it blacker. Once I finish pullin' 'em string beans and choppin' me some wood for the night's fire, I bees all tuckered out. Feels like all I wants to do is go rushin' off to bed, but I got mouths to feed, so I keep on pushin'."

That's the last thing she remembered her great-grandma saying to her. Two days later she died. "Guess it was that Alabama heat," Portia thought out loud before she turned away from the window. She walked back to the sofa and sat down. Early in the day, if the oncologist hadn't measured the section of her tumor the lumpectomy failed to cut away and told her, "The things growing," she'd be visiting her grandma.

Her grandma. The same woman who was pulling rose bushes along the side of her house two days ago when Portia drove up in her BMW. She helped Katrina dig a deep hole and plant one of the rose bushes. A scent like a modest spraying of expensive perfume rushed up her nose when she leaned toward the bush and pushed it into the ground. Half an hour later, she was washing her hands at the kitchen sink while Katrina poured them both a cup of hot apple, cinnamon tea. When she sat down, Katrina looked across the table at her and started talking. She smiled and nodded into everything Katrina said, everything except the last words Katrina spoke before she glanced at her watch and told her she had to get home.

Katrina's tea cup was empty. She circled her mouth with the end of her tongue. Then she leaned toward the center of the table and told Portia, "Don't you be scared, Portia. Child, don't you be scared about nothing. Keep on stomping, Girl. Don't you let nobody or nothing make you give up on life. Because, whether all those other folk who think they don't have anything wrong with them want to believe it or not, we're all dying. All of us are going to die. The thing I hate about what you got is that I don't want you to get to heaven ahead of me." Then she reached out and took Portia's hands inside hers. The heat from the tea cup having settled on her palms, Katrina pushed a soft, warm feeling across Portia's hands while she held them inside her own. "I love you, Baby. You're my baby girl."

Rather than visit Katrina, Portia sat on the sofa and imagined Chicagoans who suffered to the degree she now did. Homeless citizens, teenage runaways, physically abused wives and rape and child molestation victims haunted her. They taunted her for thinking she moved away from trouble the day she landed her high salaried job at Courtney & Sons, the day she bought her three-bedroom rancher, the day she paid off the loan on her BMW.

She sighed. She thought about a street lady she saw each morning while she drove to work. The lady pushed a wobbling, rusted grocery cart up and down Michigan Avenue.

She told herself if she were poor like that woman, cancer would mean nothing to her. With her back pressed so hard against the sofa she felt as if she was going to become part of the furniture, she dreamed of being poor. She pulled her legs up slowly and rested her feet on the coffee table, something she never before allowed herself or anyone else to do. She mused out loud. "If I was that street lady, I wouldn't be sitting here feeling like I have six months to live. I wouldn't know I have cancer, because I wouldn't afford doctor visits, and, like they say, what you don't know can't hurt you." Giving the idea consideration, she waved the notion out of her mind. "No. It's awful for me to think that woman's life is wishfully easier than mine. Me with a nice house and a nice car. Oh, what's it matter? We're both dying! Ain't no difference between that bag lady and me; never was. We're both dying." Dropping her feet to the floor, she sat erect. "Why can't I live a full life? Why can't I have real love from a strong, black man and be vibrant -- be full of life -- both at the same time." Her voice thinned. Her knees trembled.

She thought about suicide. Today it seemed her best cure. Shame for listing self-imposed death as a way to rid her life of pain came to her through songs. She heard the songs while she was a little girl sitting next to her mother in church. Her mother rocked to the rhythm in the music that accompanied the words to the songs. As a little, wide-eyed girl, she worked to separate the words in the songs from moans and deep grunted pleas. "Yes, Lords", "Sweet Jesuses", and "Please Gods" went up from adult parishioners and warmed her soul.

The songs said, "Hush. Hush. Somebody's calling my name. . . . Steal away. Steal away to Jesus. I ain't got long to stay here. . . . Swing low, sweet chariot, coming for to carry me home. I looked over Jordan and what did I see? Coming for to carry me home. I seen a band of angels coming after me. Coming for to carry me home." And, "When all God's children get to heaven. It's gonna be a great day! It's gonna be a great day when we all go marching home." Pushing to the edge of the sofa, she knew suicide wouldn't take her from earth to heaven.

Besides the songs, she remembered this morning she told Dennis, "I'm going to take good care of myself, Baby, the way I have since I was a little girl. I love you too much to let go of us now. This isn't going to get me. I'm not going to let it. I feel like loving you for a long, long time."

She stood and stiffened her legs. Her knees continued to shake. She walked into her bedroom and sat on the edge of her bed. It wasn't long before she was on her back watching the ceiling go around and around. "Get a hold of yourself, Portia. Girl, get a hold of yourself." Her body turned hot, and the room went black.

Twenty minutes later, she squirmed on the bed. A layer of sweat covered her body. Pulling herself up by the elbows, she dabbed at the sweat with the tips of her fingers. She was cold. She stopped in between dabs and folded her arms around her shoulders. She rocked herself from side to side. When she stopped rocking, she reached across the bed to her nightstand and picked up a pen and a note pad.

*April 18, 1985*
*Dear Mama,*

*I wish I could tell you this face to face, but I haven't the courage. I know this is going to hurt you, and you deserve better than that from me. The radiation treatments aren't working. Believe it or not, the tumor's growing. Mama, I have so many things I want to say to you. Please tell Grandpa and Grandmama Armstrong and Grandpa and Grandmama Fowler I love them. I wrote you this letter, because I know you'll answer. If it's too late to answer, you read so often, I know you'll understand. Tell Edwin and the others--Edwin always was my favorite like Deborah is yours, though you'll never admit it--I love them. My strength wanes, so this won't be long. Fortunate for you, because my head is full . . . so many memories. It's true. Your life does pass before you just before you die.*

*You'll all be sitting in the living room caroling come Christmas Day. I'll miss every one of you. Remember that dog we used to have? I think I was eight years old when we got that dog. When I was twelve I know Dad took him to the neighbor's grandparents for them to keep. Who did you two think you were fooling? We all knew. Oh, Mama, we shared so many eventful days together. Picking cherries at Grandmama Armstrong's. Those were the best cherries, and Grandmama always made me a big cobbler. She said it was all mine. Don't tell the others, but that was the best part. They had to actually ask me for a piece. The street races we ran as kids with the neighbors . . . We had such fun growing up. Remember that old Pinto Dad and you gave me after I graduated from high school? Piece of junk. Thanks anyway. That car got me to the farthest places away from home then stopped and refused to start again. I dropped twenty pounds in the two years I had that car, I had to get out and walk back home so many times. And Thanksgiving . . . Mama, remember Thanksgiving dinner at our house . . .*

Portia's grandparents crossed the street. Wet snowflakes that coated their automobile windshields during the drive from their homes to Denny and Rebecca's house fell thicker, faster. As they neared Denny and Rebecca's house, Eddie looked at the driveway. When he saw Portia, Craig, Deborah and Robert's cars, he smiled.

Katrina gazed into the falling snow before she turned and faced Priscilla. "When all the kids get here, Rebecca and Denny's place'll be packed."

Priscilla pursed her lips and shook her head. "And noisy too, Honey."

"Girl, yes."

Roger leaned so close to Priscilla, their faces brushed together. He grinned like a fox. "And ol' Miss Barnes across the street'll be fussing. Because after all the family gets here, there won't be a single parking space," he tossed his hand across his shoulder, "over there."

Turning, Priscilla looked toward the curb Roger and her, cherry/brown Ford was parked against. "Ol' Miss Barnes is just mad because she's too mean for anybody to want to park across the street and visit with her on Thanksgiving Day."

"Some of the family can park in the alley behind the garage," Katrina injected. "Speaking of Rebecca's place," her voice went up, "'Cilla, Girl, don't you like what Rebecca's done to that front walk?"

Priscilla's eyes ballooned. She guided them up the walkway. "Child, yes."

"How she took that white rock and sprinkled it up the edges of the sidewalk. I told her, come spring time, the front of her house's gonna look cute as all get out."

Priscilla smiled at the thought while she watched snow flake the sides and tops of the white rock. "Child, yes."

Though he would never understand why women talked about houses as if the men who lived in them had no hand in their upkeep, Eddie was glad Priscilla and Katrina were interested in the walkway. He figured their preoccupation with the sidewalk would allow him to discuss football with Roger without Katrina frowning out the words, "That's all you do is talk about sports."

"Roger?"

Chicago's overcast sky pushed a gust of cold wind down Roger's coat collar. He walked faster. "Yeah, Eddie?"

"The Bengals and the Steelers play today, don't they?"

Cold bumps rose on Roger's wrist when he pulled his coat sleeve back. He peered at his watch, "Right now!"

Eddie's eyes ballooned. "Now?"

Roger nodded out the word, "Yeah."

The wind whistled shrilly, and both men hurried.

No longer interested in Denny and Rebecca's front walk, Priscilla eyed Katrina and grunted. "Ump! Girl! It's like a man to watch sports every chance he gets."

Katrina shook her head. "Girl, who're you telling?"

"They glue themselves to the television screen."

Katrina nodded and picked up her pace. "Um-hmmm."

Priscilla quickened her steps. Her breath thickened. She winked at Katrina before she announced, "They want to see that football game more than they want to see their family."

When Eddie saw Katrina and Priscilla edging up on Roger and him, he moaned, "Awww."

Roger raised his voice. "You talk like we came over here just to watch the game."

"You both know better," Eddie said laughing. "Roger and I had to rush you two off the phone so we could get over here before Denny prayed Grace and cut the turkey."

Katrina batted her eyelashes. "True, but Priscilla and I know how men like watching a game with the fellahs."

Eddie arched his brow. "I forgot about the game."

"And I only thought about it once while I was reading the morning newspaper." Roger was determined not to quit while Eddie and he seemed, for the first time in more than thirty years, to be ahead.

Pursing her lips and narrowing her brow, Priscilla cooed, "Sure, Roger."

Roger waved his hand. "You two are just trying to start some mess."

Priscilla and Katrina pulled their coat collars up around their necks and laughed so hard they failed to see Robert standing in the storm door.

"Grandparents."

Eddie looked up. "Robert, why are you grinning so hard?"

Roger tugged on the ends of his coat sleeves. "And not inviting us in from out of this cold?"

When she overheard her grandfathers' voices from her place on the sofa, Deborah echoed their wishes, "Robert, let them in."

With a furrowed brow, Robert turned and looked over his shoulder. "I am, Deborah."

"Well, do it."

Robert jerked his shoulders and faced his sister, "Girl, if you don't shut up."

Katrina pulled on the storm door. "Child, step back and open this door."

Robert obliged, "Yes, Ma'am."

From where she stood leaning against the arch that separated the living room from the dining room, Rebecca watched the storm door swing open. When her gaze crossed her parents' faces, she uncrossed her arms and raised her voice, "Mama!"

Katrina neared Rebecca with opened arms, "Happy Thanksgiving, Baby!"

Rebecca waved over Katrina's shoulder at Eddie. "Hi, Daddy!"

Eddie walked close to her and squeezed the end of her hand. "Hi, Baby. Happy Thanksgiving."

"How have Mama and you been, Daddy?"

"Fine, Honey, just fine."

"Great." She stepped back and looked at her mother's tall, slender frame. "Mama, you look good as usual." A second later, she looked over her shoulder at her father again. "You both do."

Katrina stepped back, out of Rebecca's embrace, and teased, "Of course, we do."

Eddie sat in Denny's favorite lounge chair. "So, like I was saying, what's been going on?"

Denny walked next to the stereo, and, reaching to the wall, he turned the heat up. "Same ol', same ol'."

"That's good." Eddie watched Denny's arm move. A second later he called out, "Rebecca?"

"Dad?"

"What's been happening with you?"

"Mostly school." She smiled. "You know I like to teach."

"That's good, Rebecca," Katrina interjected. "Sit down. Rest Girl. I want to talk with you about something a little later."

Leaving her place under the arch, Rebecca crossed the room and sat on the sofa next to Katrina. "What?"

In an instant, Katrina presumed ignorant, "What?"

"Yes, what?" Rebecca leaned forward on the sofa and chuckled at her mother's attempt at innocence. "What did you want to talk with me about?"

"Oh," Katrina waved her hand. "Self-publishing a book of poetry."

"Self publishing is expensive, Mama."

"Rest, Baby. You've been working hard. We can talk about it later." She crossed her legs. "Did all your brothers and sisters say they were coming over for Thanksgiving dinner this year?"

The living room noisy with chatter, sitting across from Katrina, Deborah and Ressey raised their voices.

Ressey pulled her brown, pleated skirt over her knees and crossed her legs. "Girl, did you check out that Brother at Swanks last night?"

Deborah arched her brow. "The Brother in the black leather pants?"

Ressey chuckled. "The tight, black leather pants."

Deborah sat back in her chair and laughed. "Ew. Yes. I saw him."

"Was his body working overtime or what? I mean, Girl. That man was too fine!"

"He was, but he had a roving eye."

Ressey twisted her mouth. "How did you tell that in one night? Deborah, if you don't stop thinking every man is a skirt chaser, you are never going to find a good man. You wouldn't recognize one if he was standing right smack dab in front of you."

"I would. I just know that most men are about games."

"Not all—"

"I don't have time for games."

"Well," she chuckled. "Was the Brother fine or what?"

Deborah laughed. "Yeah. He was fine. Made me wish his gaze would stop rolling from you to me to Karen to Monica to Lisa to—"

"Girl, stop."

At 3:58 in the evening on November 28, 1975, the three-story, red brick house located at 1231 Willshire Avenue in Chicago,

Illinois, the house Portia, her sisters, brothers, mother and father laughed, cried, prayed, sang and danced in, was filled with loud music and laughter. An enticing aroma went from the kitchen through the chimney a long way down the street.

Portia's toddler aged nieces and nephews bounced on the tips of their toes in Portia and her sister's former bedroom. "Miss Mary Mack, Mack, Mack, all dressed in black, black, black. She asked her mother, mother, mother for fifteen cents, cents, cents. To see the elephant, elephant, elephant jump the fence, fence, fence..."

"Carolyn?"

Carolyn swung her hips from side to side. "What, Monica?"

"You and Joyce stop clapping and singing so we can think up some games to play."

"Miss Mary Mack, Mack, Mack, all dressed in black, black, black. She asked her mother, mother, mother . . . "

Lona's temple veins pulsed. "Joyce!" Lona screamed at her sister until she stopped clapping, "Listen to Monica. She's older than you like I am. And I know you're going to be wanting to play a game later."

In a show of defiance, Joyce blinked her eyes, "So."

"So, let's think up some games to play now, so later you won't be whining, 'I'm bored.'"

"Miss Mary Mack, Mack, Mack . . . "

Motown hits spun on the phonograph next to the freezer in a corner of the basement. At the foot of the basement stairs, Portia kicked up her heels and laughed. While she laughed, she turned her feet in circles. "Anne, Girl, yes."

Sensing the rise of hard laughter in Portia, Anne continued with, "And, Girl, that was only the beginning."

Leaning forward on her seat atop the chest once stuffed with school clothes and now crammed with hammers, nails, screw drivers and one chain saw, Bonnie crossed her legs and intercepted her sister, Anne's story. "Portia. When Anne came home at 2 o'clock in the morning, Mama was waiting."

"No!" Deborah knew what was next.

Anne told the remainder of the story. "You know how Mama says, 'It's all right, Girl. Go out and have yourself a good time,' when we ask if we can go out on a date, then just before we hit the door she adds, 'Just be home by midnight.' I didn't want to go anyhow. The dude was one of Bonnie's friend's partners." She rolled her eyes and waved her hand. "And, Girl . . ."

Janice rocked on the last basement step and laughed. "Bonnie's old man hung out with some characters, didn't he? Bonnie had nerve enough to try and fix me up with one of those jokers."

Faye ran her hand across her forehead. "Don't I know."

Bonnie defended her choice in men. "They weren't that bad. Frank and Paul were good men."

When Ressey shifted on the clothes dryer, it shook and clanged. "Go ahead, Anne."

"Mama was sitting on the bed when I came up the front walk. I know because her night light was on. I saw her shadow as soon as we turned the corner, even before I got out of that raggedy piece of junk he kept patting the dashboard of and calling his ride. I ran up to the door. I had my key in my hand. I didn't want him trying to kiss me. He did and I slapped him. But he only got to me because Mama put the chain lock on. I couldn't get in. I banged and banged on the front door. I didn't dare scream. I didn't want Mama tearing into my behind. When she came down and unlocked the door, the first thing she said was, 'It's two o'clock in the morning. I told you to be in by midnight, didn't I?'" Anne shook her head. "What a night, I had a three hour date with a player. He ate. We went to Chicken Fix, of all places to take a date, and he sucked down six--six, Girls--pieces of chicken. At the movie, Boost, he kept telling me how people wouldn't stop telling him he looked like the actor, Jerome Michaels." Her face brightened. "You know how fine Jerome Michaels is. With his pretty, brown eyed self. But that player I was with--" She waved her hand and pursed her lips. "Ask me, he favored the pot-bellied taxi cab driver on the sitcom, Gloria's. And after all that chicken eating he did, when I got home, Mama chewed my behind for what I know had to be half an hour."

Cynthia exclaimed, "We'll have to warn our daughters to beware of players."

Portia raised her shoulders. "Not me. I'm not getting married or having kids. A man has nothing to do with how I'm going to meet my mortgage, pay my car note or clothe and feed myself. I don't need a man to be happy or to survive."

"Well, of course you don't need anybody, Portia." Anne laughed. "You're the child who birthed herself."

Nearer the freezer, Portia's brothers and male cousins sat in old musty chairs and on one twenty-year-old sofa.

Bo cleared his throat. "Yeah? How long did you play ball, Lewis?"

"All through grade school, junior high and high school."

"Yeah?"

One of the rusted safety pins holding a dusty cushion to the arm of the sofa snapped open and stuck Lewis in the side when he turned to face his cousin. "Ew!" Taking the point of the safety pin away from his skin, he sat forward on the sofa. "Yeah, Man."

Stanley, taller and bulkier than his younger brother, Bo, narrowed his eyes, and pushed to the sofa's edge. "Yeah."

Though Bo saw Stanley get jealous before, especially during the fourth quarter of a football game Jefferson was losing badly, each time he witnessed Stanley's envy, a chill went up his spine. He waved his hand. "It's cool, Stanley. I just asked." Then he turned in the chair and faced Lewis, "Running back, Man?"

"No. Fullback. I've always been this big."

"You got pumped after you finally stopped running from bully, Keith, and kicked his butt in the fifth grade. You were fat before then."

"Yeah. But now I'm the man."

"Running those bleachers at school did make you quick, smooth."

"Finesse, Man, finesse. I used to burst up the line, around the line, intercept . . . Man, I did it all. Yesss. Yesss. Yes, Sir. I was bad, Man . . . too tough to stop."

Robert shook his head. "Awww, talk about fast and smooth, I rushed over 1000 yards a season three years in a row."

"Days gone by. I'm doing my thing now." Edwin stood from his place center sofa, and, jogging in place until his knees reached above his waist, he looked from the sofa to the old chairs at each of his cousins and brothers.

Thomas grinned. He gripped the end of Edwin's right hand and pulled it twice. "Say, what?"

"Doing my thing now, Thomas."

"High stepping, Brother."

Thomas snapped his fingers and let the word, "Yeah," drag from his mouth.

Stanley leaned against the back of the chair he sat in until it squeaked. Sticking his hand to the bottom of his pant pocket, he pulled out a piece of hard orange candy. "Who'd Jefferson play this season? Anybody tough? And yeah, Thomas, how'd Jefferson do in the tournament?" He unwrapped the candy, "We'll see how good the team was this year."

Gary waved his hand. "Awww, Man, your name's not on the board in the gym."

Stanley's tongue made a clucking noise when he sucked the candy. "The board inside the trophy case?"

Gary nodded, "That board."

Pursing his lips and turning on the sofa, Robert looked at Stanley. He wore a sheepish grin. "Un-hunh."

Hoping to escape embarrassment, Stanley iterated, "That board?" Then he squirmed and sucked the candy. "Awww, I had some off days."

Laughter buzzed in Stanley's ears while he dug to the bottom of his pant pocket, hunting another piece of candy.

"Some off days, hunh?"

Still digging in his pant pocket, Stanley grinned like a fox. "Yeah."

"No, Man." Gary said. "You all know I was picking at Stanley. He was boss when he played ball for Jefferson." When he sat erect, he and Stanley slapped palms.

Still searching for an answer, Stanley repeated, "So, who'd Jefferson play this year?"

Thomas answered, "We had two easy games and that was Wright and Smithson."

"Who else did you play?"

"Tipson, Rodgers, Fayette, Hyatt . . . "

Upon hearing Tipson and Rodgers, Stanley raised his hand. "That's enough, Thomas." He pursed his lips and shook his head. "I know Jefferson played some ball this year."

Thomas grinned. "That's what I've been trying to tell you."

Edwin added, "We beat 'em all. Squashed 'em like they were cock roaches!"

Brothers and cousins slapped one another's palms. Their laughter boomeranged off the concrete basement walls and created such a racket, no one heard Rebecca's footsteps approach the top of the stairs. She called out in a loud voice, "Come on!" In a moment, the basement was empty.

Paul stared at the turkey, ham, raisin and honey ginger bread loaves, homemade dinner rolls, boiled cabbage seasoned with a can of corn beef, cole slaw and tossed salad. He ran his tongue around his mouth when his gaze fell across the deviled eggs, spinach, black eyed peas, broccoli covered with cheddar cheese, yams, mashed potatoes and creamy white gravy, dressing, baked macaroni and cheese, collard greens, cherry cheese cake, peach cobbler, orange juice and soda.

Rebecca glanced around the table. "Why's everyone sitting still?" She wore a smirk. "Dinner's buffet style this year." When no one moved, she chuckled and added, "You know, serve yourself?"

Denny reached to the center of the table and grabbed a serving spoon.

"Dad, do you want me to pass you the mashed potatoes?" Faye chuckled out loud while she glanced at the mashed potatoes that plopped down on the tablecloth instead of on Denny's plate.

Denny eyed her graciously. "Please."

"Sure."

"Rebecca?"

Rebecca turned until she faced her sister, Trish. "Yea, Sis?"

"Cut me a slice of that hard butter, please."

The butter stuck to the end of the knife Rebecca held in her hand. "Here."

Trish reached across the table from where she sat two chairs down from Rebecca, "Thanks."

When Thomas looked at the slice of hard butter, he turned up his nose. "You like hard butter?"

Trish pressed the butter against a slice of raisin bread. "Yes."

"It takes so long to melt."

Trish sat the knife on the edge of her plate. "I don't want it to melt."

Edwin leaned back in his chair until its front legs raised off the floor. He gulped his soda. At six feet and ten inches tall, Deborah proclaimed him tallest in their family. "Aunt Lillian!"

Lillian, shortest and plumpest in the family and always on a diet, called back to Edwin as loudly as he called to her, "What?" She paused, "Edwin, was that you?"

Edwin sipped on the cola before he answered. "Yes."

Lillian leaned toward the table. After she stopped gazing at the baked macaroni and cheese and homemade rolls, she said, "It's hard telling who's who around here anymore." She leaned against the spine of her chair and laughed until the rows of fat on her stomach jiggled. Her breath smelled of strong liquor. "There are so many of us." She slapped the tabletop. "Just look at this dining room and the younger ones in the kitchen." She shook her head. "I don't know how this family does it, but each year it gets bigger." She peered at Rebecca, "Pretty soon you're not going to be able to fit all of us in your house, Sis." She shook her head again. "Ump. Ump."

Katrina interjected, "That means we'll have to have Thanksgiving dinner at Bill and your house for the first time ever next year."

Lillian retorted. "No. That means Rebecca and Denny'll have to sale this house and buy a larger one. That or my baby Portia's gonna have to hurry and get married, so we can all go to her house on Thanksgiving." She pressed her spine against the chair's cushion and laughed.

Katrina lowered her head before she shook it. "Lillian, you're a mess. You're just lazy. As much as you eat, I know you can cook, Girl."

"Mama, stop talking about my weight."

"I'm not talking about your weight. If you would've let me finish, you would've heard me say, I wish you'd cook Thanksgiving dinner just once. I don't know why you haven't had Thanksgiving dinner at your house, you or your sisters." She waved her hand. "You know you can cook. I taught all of you girls how to cook."

Edwin raised his voice. "Aunt Lillian, do you think you can get me a job at the hospital this summer?"

She looked straight ahead, "A full-time job?"

Edwin nodded and sat his chair's front legs on the floor. "Yes."

Lillian reached across the table and took a large helping of macaroni and cheese. "Is this job only for the summer?" She glanced at Rebecca and Denny.

"No. Since I graduate this year, I want to get a head start on the other high school seniors who'll be out job hunting."

Trish's husband, George picked up two hot dinner rolls. "Good. Smart strategy. You'll get a job. I'll check the board at the factory for you. Besides, I know you'd like to have your own place." He chuckled. "That's the first thing I wanted after I graduated from high school. I wanted to move out, move out, move out."

"Now you're going to tell him how hard it was to pay the bills once you got out on your own." Sharon, George's youngest cousin, furrowed her brow. "Grown folk're always trying to discourage teenagers."

George chuckled. "No. That's not what I was going to say. In fact, I wasn't going to say another word. But, you're right. Young folk get discouraged too much, but I don't think I do that."

Sharon almost apologized. "No. You don't do that. I shouldn't have said that."

"That's okay." George peered at Thelma, his aunt and Sharon's mother. "I know how well some daughters got along with their mothers when they were teenagers."

"Sharon and I got by."

Rebecca waved her hand, as if pushing Thelma, George and Sharon's words aside. "Oh, stop all of this nonsense. I want to eat. You all can argue later, but I wish you wouldn't. You three argue almost every time you get together. It's reached the point that whenever you're in a room together, I expect you to argue. So, save it. I'm hungry." She turned and looked down the table at Denny and nodded.

Denny pushed his hands to the table's edge. When he saw everyone's plate full with food, he folded his hands in his lap and bowed his head. Forks and spoons stilled. All pairs of hands circling the table came together and folded. Everyone's head was hung. "Let's say grace. Lord, thank you. You have been good. Here we are, as a family, assembled together again. Our circle is unbroken. We have good jobs, good health and good love from our family and our friends. We have our wise matriarchs and patriarchs with us. We have toddlers in the kitchen. We have a roof over our heads and joy in our hearts. None of us is in pain. None of us is sick. Lord, thank you. Please, bless the food we are about to enjoy. Bless those who prepared it in love. Lord, we also ask that you bless and guide us to make the wisest decisions, with your Holy Spirit, as we go about our days, on our jobs and in our separate homes. I pray in Jesus' mighty name, and, thank you, Lord, for, through faith, we know we have what we ask for. Amen."

Portia lifted her head, turned, smiled and winked at her Aunt Lillian.. "Amen."

Thomas lifted his head and unfolded his hands. "Amen."

Katrina nodded before she stabbed a pile of seasoned collard greens with her fork. "Edwin, Bo and Thomas, how's school coming?"

Edwin nodded. "Fine, Grandma Armstrong."

"And you, Thomas?"

"Fine."

She looked at Bo. "Bo?"

Bo nodded and swallowed a fork full of broccoli. "Fine, Grandmama."

"That's good. You three are the only kids left in high school, aren't you?"

"Yes, Ma'am," Edwin answered.

She chewed her collard greens. "These kids are growing so fast, aren't they, Rebecca?"

Rebecca swallowed a spoonful of macaroni and cheese. She wiped her mouth before she answered, "You know it."

Katrina picked up another fork full of collard greens. "Girl, I remember when you first started cooking these Thanksgiving dinners."

With her mouth full of dark turkey, Rebecca tipped her head toward her mother.

Katrina reached over and nudged her daughter Rebe's elbow. "Remember how scared Rebecca was?"

"She didn't trust anything she cooked."

Rebecca tipped her head again.

"Look at her, Trish."

"I see her, Mama."

"The turkey's too dry. I know you all don't like the food. You're just saying you like it, so you won't hurt my feelings. I burned the rolls. Look. They're too dark. They're burnt." Katrina sat her fork on her plate and laughed.

Chewing last bits of the turkey, Rebecca waved her hand and dropped her bottom lip. "Oh, Mama, stop."

"Remember how she was, Denny?"

"Who're you telling. That woman worried me and herself sick. She always took two alka seltzer after you all cleared out."

"Did she?"

"Yes, Ma'am."

Rebecca wiped turkey crumbs from the corners of her mouth; the pout remained. "Well."

Katrina laughed into, "Look at her. She started believing she was a good cook after she cooked her third Thanksgiving dinner. She told me . . . Then Portia and the other kid's friends started asking to visit around dinnertime. They wanted to eat her cooking. She knew she was a chef then."

Edwin tried again. "Aunt Lillian?"

She chewed on a dinner roll. "What, Baby?"

"Can you get me a job?"

She sipped her ice water. "It'll probably have to be in housekeeping, but I can get you a job." She nodded. "Sure. I can get you a job. The turnover in the housekeeping department is one of the highest in the hospital. You might not be wild about the job, but it'll pay you enough, and it's not all that bad." She took another sip of her ice water. "All in all, I think you'll enjoy working at the hospital. I know it'll be nice having you working there. Some days we can eat lunch together and chat. You know, hang out." She laughed at the idea of having lunch with him, catching up on family news. "When do you want to start?"

He swallowed a mouthful of candied yams. "As soon as possible."

"All right." She eyed Rebecca and Denny before she stuffed her mouth with boiled cabbage. "Rebecca and Denny, you two don't have anything to do with this, do you?"

Denny answered. "No. You know we taught our children to be independent, and they are. Rebecca and I are proud of that. I'm glad Edwin wants to get a job, but we didn't force him to go job hunting. We raised him to want a job. What's wrong with that?"

"Just as long as he doesn't turn out as serious as Portia. She's my baby, but that girl thinks too much."

Portia glanced up at her aunt.

She winked at Portia before she said, "You do."

"Leave Portia alone, Lil. She's not bothering you. You might try minding your own business like she does so much of the time. And what's wrong with thinking and being independent? Wanting to make a go of things on your own?"

Lillian bowed and shook her head. "Nothing. There's nothing wrong with that. That's how Bill and I raised our kids. I'm all for that. Portia's grown now. She's nothing going to change. But, Edwin. I just thought it strange that a high school senior would be job hunting now. He's not even out of school yet. And you yourself know how you have to twist kids arms to get them to work, especially around the house."

Priscilla interjected, "Don't I know it. I had a time getting Denny to dust furniture when he was a boy." She shook her head. "I had a time."

"Mama."

"Un-un. Getting you to clean up around the house was like pulling teeth. It was a job. I'd rather to clean up myself than fight with you to dust one coffee table, but I had to teach you responsibility." She waved her hand, reached across the table, and cut herself a slice of honey gingerbread. "You were a mess."

"I wasn't that bad."

"Oh, yes you were." She spoke with a raised finger, "As a matter of fact, you were the hardest to get to help out around the house. You'd rather take a beating."

Tugging on his pant belt, Denny surrendered. "Okay, okay, Mama. I didn't like to do housework, but I helped outside in the yard and on the farm. Pops'll tell you that. You know that. I just didn't like cleaning house. I help out around here though." He chuckled, "Rebecca'd kick my butt if I didn't."

Priscilla winked at Rebecca. "That 'ah woman."

Two seats down from Priscilla, Rebe leaned forward and rested her elbows on the edge of the table. She picked her teeth with the tip of her tongue. "Lillian, remember that time you worked at that radio station? You were a secretary then. I came to pick you up and my truck broke down?"

Lillian's eyes ballooned. She nibbled a slice of raisin bread. "Don't I remember!" She threw the bread on her plate. "That was a scary night. I thought I was going to pee on myself. While we walked further and further away from your broke down truck, I kept hearing myself breath, and, Girl, I didn't know who it was." She laughed. "I kept thinking someone was following us while we walked to Bill and my apartment." She shook her head. "What a night. Ump. Ump. I don't ever want to experience that again."

Trish arched her brow. "What night was this? You two never told..." She turned and looked at Rebecca. "Rebecca and me."

Rebe giggled into her cupped palms. "We forgot."

Lillian sat tall in her chair. "We didn't want you to tell Mama or Dad. We ran like mad once we reached the corner of the intersection the radio station was on. We probably could have won an Olympic gold medal as fast as we were running." She nudged Rebe's elbow. "We were getting it, weren't we, Girl?"

Rebe laughed until she had to stop and catch her breath. "We sure were. I haven't run that fast since that night. Whew! It was dark outside. What a night for my truck to break down. I had it for nine years. Nine years, now that's a long time to own a truck. I got seven good years out of it." She chuckled. "The last two years were the pits." Then she turned and looked at Lillian. "I didn't go back and get that truck, did I?"

Trish interrupted. "You must not have. I know I never saw that truck again, that ugly ol' truck."

Rebe pouted. "Stop talking about my truck."

Lillian sat back in her chair bug-eyed. "You mean to tell me you're going to defend that truck? That raggedy truck gave us a terrible scare that night." She leaned closer to the center of the table and whispered, "Remember those two guys we saw, Rebe?"

Rebecca opened her mouth. "What two guys?"

"One guy wore a hat big enough to be a sombrero. The other guy wore this . . ." Lillian twisted her mouth. "I don't know." She threw her hands in the air. "He had a hat pulled down over his right ear, like he was trying to be cool or something. They both looked out of place. Seeing them was what scared me most. I thought they were following us. We went down a block, they went down a block. We turned a corner; they turned a corner. It was eerie." She bowed her head before she shook it. "I think they followed us for fifteen minutes. Finally, I turned around and they weren't behind us anymore." She sat back in her chair. "Rebe, you remember those two guys?" She arched her brow. "Don't you?"

Rebe scowled. "I guess I remember, but they're not real clear to me now. I don't remember any hats. Doesn't mean they weren't wearing hats though. I just don't remember hats."

"Well, they were wearing hats."

"I believe you, Lil. I just don't remember any hats."

Trish stuck her fingernail between her teeth. "Well, I'm glad you both can talk about something a couple of minutes without fighting. Because, Child, you two sure fought when we were kids."

"That's only because Rebe told everything we did to Mama and Dad. That girl had us getting more beatings, and me most of all. I got more beatings than all of the rest of you put together." Lillian's eyes bulged. "And I had to share a bed with her." She shook her head. "Mama and Dad wanted Rebe and me to be the best of friends. I guess they got what they wanted, because after Rebe graduated from junior high, you couldn't separate us."

Trish leaned forward. "And aren't I glad. You two fought like cats and dogs, especially after you climbed into bed. It took an hour for you two to settle into bed, shut up, and fall to sleep." She pursed her lips. "Then Lillian would start snoring. There were nights when I wondered if I was ever going to fall to sleep on account of you two. You fought over who had the most cover, who was sleeping on more of the bed than the other, and on and on you'd go. You were too much."

Rebe waved her hand. "Oh, well."

Rebecca agreed. "Yes. Oh, well. So, what do you girls have planned for next weekend?" While she listened to her sisters relay their plans, she watched Denny push his chair away from the table and run his tongue across his teeth.

"So, how's retirement these days, Dad? Still sweet?"

Eddie sat back in his chair and patted his stomach. He belched before he grinned. "Well, now, let's see. I usually get up around seven. Sometimes I treat Katrina to breakfast."

Priscilla winked at Katrina.

"I do. After she leaves for work, I fool around in the house. I'll read a novel or ride the exercise bike. You know, just something. Later in the day, sometimes I go fishing or boating. All my kids know how I enjoy the water." He tapped the point of Denny's elbow. "Like you." Then he smiled and continued, "Sometimes I take my ten speed out of the basement and ride on the neighborhood bike trail. I keep busy. I enjoy retirement. I worked two full-time jobs for over twenty years." His face stretched into a long smile. "Retirement's always going to be sweet for me."

Denny unfastened his belt. When he did, his stomach went out like a balloon. "Maybe I ought to retire."

Eddie tightened his brow and pointed his thoughts at Denny. "You're not old enough."

Priscilla, never one for minding her own business, stopped waving her hands and batting her eyelashes. "Ain't that the truth."

"I could retire if I had a few ten more thousand dollars saved."

"What about your pension?" Eddie refused to turn Denny loose from reality.

"I'd get that in time." Raising his voice, he admitted, "I know I can't retire right now. It's just a thought that keeps me going. One day I'll be able to retire. I just hope I enjoy retirement as much as you do, Dad."

Eddie smiled thinly at Denny while he clasped his hands together and sat them on the table. "I wasn't trying to bust your bubble, Son. I was just telling it like it is. Economists say it takes more money to retire with each passing generation. And frankly, I don't think Social Security's going to hold out much longer. I heard the program's having major trouble. Money makes people do foolish things. I think a lot of the Social Security money has been misused. I'm not the only one who thinks so either. But, you'll retire, Son. And you'll enjoy it. Yes," his head started nodding. "You'll enjoy it. You'll enjoy being retired as much as I have, if not more. I can tell. You've been working a mighty long time. Like I did. You're a working man, but you're ready to give some of that hard labor up. Believe me, I know the feeling. I felt the same way for about five years before I retired. I know how you feel, and I don't blame you. Hang in there another seven to ten years though. Hang in there."

As if to relax her family's growing bellies and expanding thoughts, Rebecca pushed her chair away from the table. "Let's play a game, work off these calories."

"What game?"

Rebecca turned with a shrug and looked at her sister. "I don't know, Trish." A second later, she popped her fingers. "Spaddle! We had a blast when we played Spaddle last Christmas. Remember?"

"Spaddle?" Roger drew up his nose.

Denny nodded. "All right. I suppose."

Priscilla stopped talking fast and turned away from Katrina. She arched her shoulders. "Sure."

Eddie wasn't contrary. "Why not?"

"It looks like Spaddle's the game." Rebecca stood.

Denny walked in Rebecca's footsteps. He didn't stop following her until he reached the first empty living room chair he saw. Extending his legs, he sat with an "unh!"

Recalling Christmas, the last time Rebecca suggested the family play Spaddle, Katrina couldn't help asking, "Where's the game?" She didn't want to spend two hours hunting for a game Rebecca forgot she threw in the garbage on the same day she did her spring-cleaning.

Turning at the foot of the living room stairs, Rebecca waved at Katrina. "Oh, Mama, I'll get it."

"Sure?"

"Want help?" Denny asked reluctantly while Rebecca hurried upstairs.

Because she heard the hesitancy in his voice, Rebecca answered, "No. I'll find it myself," as quickly as she walked. She braced the banister and jogged to the top of the carpeted stairs. "I'll be back."

All four blue and white checkered sofa pillows circled Katrina's backside when she sat and released a deep breath, "All that for a game."

"We should just go outside and play in the snow."

Denny gawked at Eddie. "You must've lost your mind."

Priscilla added, "I'm for a trek in the snow."

"How long has it been since you've played in the snow, Mama?" Beatrice grinned, because she figured thirty years passed since either of her parents romped through the snow.

A heavy sigh was the most Priscilla gave for an answer.

"Surely, not that long, 'Scilla."

"Roger, I don't know."

She shook a pointed finger at Roger. "Remember that time when we were dating and I slid right there in front of the church? You remember that church, the A.M.E. church? We use to go every Sunday. I enjoyed those church services, but I fell right there in front of the church. Remember?" She tapped Roger's hand. "You remember that time I fell in front of the church?" Sitting against the back of the sofa, she scanned every face in the living room. "I was so embarrassed."

Roger grinned before he nodded. "I remember. My friends kept asking me if you were okay."

She pursed her mouth. "I didn't like them."

"They did ask me a lot of questions about you. But remember how you were a barracuda in those days?"

"Not to you."

Roger pulled himself to the edge of the chair he sat in and eyed her with disbelief. "Sometimes you were."

She waved her hand. "Oh. I was not."

"Never mind all that," Eddie injected. "Once Katrina and I got stuck in nine feet of snow." Wiggling until he found the lounge chair's most comfortable spot, he patted his stomach twice.

Priscilla waved her hand again. "Get out of here."

To which Katrina exclaimed, "We did!"

Priscilla needed proof. "When?"

"Ahhh. Girl, I don't remember the exact date." Katrina frowned. "It was sometime in February. 1947 wasn't it, Eddie?"

"That's when it was, February 1947. It was crazy cold. They didn't have CBs then. We were just stuck. I thought we were never going to be found. It was a good thing, a real good thing, Katrina threw that blanket into the back seat before we left the apartment." He tossed his head back. "We called ourselves going sightseeing. We were going to see how Chicago looked with its ground covered in snow. That's what we set out to do. We saw some of the city streets covered in snow all right. It's funny, now that I think about it. We huddled so close in that station wagon, trying with all our might to keep warm. When I bought my CB five years ago, I thought about that night Katrina and I got stuck in the snow. Nothing was going to stop me from getting that CB."

"You think that's funny?" Katrina chuckled. "I think the time we went sliding around on that lake was too much."

Roger crossed his legs. "What happened?"

"After about five minutes of sliding around, Eddie fell clear through."

The living room was noisy with laughter. The memory most real to him, Eddie slapped his knee and rocked while he laughed.

Priscilla's eyes swelled. "All the way through the ice and into the water?"

Katrina choked her laughter and nodded at Priscilla. "All the way through the ice and into the water."

Priscilla scooted to the edge of the sofa, leaned and patted Eddie's knee. "You poor thing."

"No. No. It was cold, but we had a good time that night. When we got back to our one room flat, Katrina ran me a hot bubble bath, and, after I climbed out of the tub, she gave me a nice back rub."

"Did the pipes in your flat freeze up after a hard snow?" Roger grinned. "Ours did."

Katrina nodded. "Yes. Yes. Yes, they sure did. It was cold as dickens in that place in the wintertime. I kept a wool coat on and a blanket wrapped around me January and February. So did Eddie."

"Roger and I stayed wrapped up in wintertime too. Back then, Chicago got cold as all get out in late January and early . . . well, all of February. Roger and I made sure we were cozy though. We hugged all the time." Priscilla's eyes brightened. "All our children were conceived in the winter."

Roger and Priscilla's youngest son, George, leaned against his wife, Samantha's shoulder. "Reminds me of our first apartment."

Samantha, a laconic woman who never laughed enough, leaned forward, braced her knees with her hands and turned a crooked grin. "I think everybody's first place was an apartment."

George tittered. "That's true, but ours had to be the ugliest apartment in America." He looked around the room. "The stains on the walls must have been part of the original marble. Those stains were on the walls deep and hard."

Samantha piped, "Marble! That wasn't marble. Those walls were made of paper. Those walls had more cracks, holes and chips in them than anything I've seen. I hated that apartment. And remember? We used milk crates for furniture. We slept on the floor. Trish, you know those milk crates the milkman used to sit milk on front porches in? When we were young, I think everybody ordered milk." Tossing her head back, she surprised everyone when she filled the room with laughter. "Maybe George and I weren't the only ones using those milk crates for furniture. I just threw some sheets over the crates. And, you know; it looked all right. None of our company ever said anything. No one ever complained. My mama never said anything." She leaned forward. "Can you believe that? My mama was the pickiest woman on earth. Yes, she was. But she didn't say a word, and she visited often, too often -- four days a week." She lowered her voice and sat back on the sofa. "She was a good woman though."

George glanced at her. "Yeah, and we had a serious case of cock roaches. You know some of those roaches could fly."

The living room exploded in laughter.

George raised his voice above the ring of laughter. "I remember. The first time I saw a flying cock roach, I called Samantha. She was standing over the stove in the kitchen . . ."

"Cooking."

George stopped long enough to look at Trish, "Yes."

"It figures. In those days, women cooked all the time."

Katrina gave Trish a hush-your-mouth-girl look, "Oh, well. Go ahead, George."

Trish narrowed her brow. "Well, they did, Mama."

Katrina sat back in disbelief. "And you don't think I know that? Right now I want to hear George's story."

Trish leaned closer to George and crossed her arms tightly.

"So, I called her, and she didn't really pay me any mind. She thought I was just talking. So I raised my voice. I said, Samantha, there's a cock roach in here, and it's flying."

The living room exploded in laughter again.

"When she came in the living room which was also our den, our dining room and our bedroom . . ."

Priscilla nodded through her laughter. "Yeah. Just like our place."

"Well, when she saw that flying cock roach, I took one look at her face and thought she was going to fall out. Her eyes were so big, they looked like golf balls."

Samantha chuckled.

"And you see how little her eyes normally are." He turned and looked at Samantha. "How long did it take me to catch that cock roach?"

She shook her head. She no longer smiled. "I don't know, but it seemed like all night."

"It was cold in the wintertime in there too."

She faced George. "Wasn't it, though?"

Lillian arched her brow. "All of those one room flats were cold in the wintertime, because Bill and mine's was too. And, you know, when we were in our late teens and early twenties, we always had the nerve to go outside and play in the snow then come back in that flat and try to get warm."

Laughter echoed in the living room when Rebecca bounded down the stairs carrying the rattling game box. No one saw her. No one except Denny's brother, Ronald, heard her feet land on the steps. He cleared his throat and offered, "I don't think anyone wants to play the game."

Rebecca stood on the last stair with the game box in her hand. She didn't move until she saw Portia, her siblings and her cousins enter the living room.

"Where are you all going?"

Paul answered first. "Out in the snow, Granddad Armstrong."

Ronald sat erect in his chair. "Rebecca?"

"Uh-huh?" Rebecca's voice deepened. Her face was long.

"While you were upstairs hunting for the game, we got to talking about how much fun we had playing in the snow years ago. I guess, like Paul said, everyone might want to go outside in the snow."

"Instead of play the game?" Rebecca held the box in one hand. Her other hand rested on her backside. Her face was tight.

Ronald nodded slowly. "Yeah."

It was her niece Tina's voice that took Rebecca's thoughts away from the game. "Mama!"

Carolyn viewed the stairs and looked behind the spot Rebecca occupied. "What, Tina?"

"What're you all talking about down there?"

"Going out in the snow."

"There's a lot of snow on the ground?"

"Yes."

"Can we go out in it?"

"Tell your cousins to come downstairs and we'll see."

Rebecca stood close to the banister while the kids ran passed her down the stairs and into the living room. When all the kids were in the living room, she sighed. "You mean to tell me, I've looked for this game for twenty minutes and not one of you wants to play it?"

Tina, nine, Gloria, ten, and Michael, eight, laughed when they looked up into their Aunt Rebecca's face.

Roger leaned back in his chair. "Sorry, Rebecca. Looks like we changed our minds."

Rebecca shook her head and watched Sophia fasten her eyes on Edwin. A finger dangled in her mouth, "Where go-in', Unc-le Ed-in?"

Edwin bent and kissed Sophia's small forehead. "Outside to play, Sweetheart."

"Can go?" Sophia pressed her finger against her chest.

Rebecca still held the game. "So, that's what everyone wants to do?"

Roger grinned. "That's what everyone wants to do."

"Rather than play the game?"

It was Roger. "Rather than play the game."

Rebecca walked into the living room and tossed the game on top of the stereo. "Let's go outside then!"

# Chapter 9

## Hospital Visits

If not for her scheduled mastectomy, Portia would still be in bed, her head resting against her pillow, her thoughts all across her bedroom. She awoke twice during the night. She went away from sleep for good at 4:30. She watched sunlight flicker and move on the ceiling. A smile tugged at the corners of her mouth while she watched the bright shapes jump, bob, weave and shimmy across the top of the room. She imagined the bright "ain't gonna be still" shapes to be her sisters, women she spent her childhood jumping rope, playing hopscotch, marbles and jacks with.

"They always said I was too serious, thought too much," she mused to herself. "Now all I have time to do is think." She looked across the room. Localized treatments. Time. Spreading cancer cells. Time. Death. What was there not to think about, she almost asked out loud. A second later, she smiled. "Thank you," she whispered to God. Then she turned her head until her gaze fell across the latest medical text she bought from the bookstore.

When she sat up, she pulled her legs over the side of the bed. Her feet brushed the shag carpet. She pushed herself off the bed and walked to the dresser mirror. Fear slowed her steps. She gripped the corner of her nightgown and pulled it away from her left breast. Her breast wasn't lumpy or sore when she touched it. A purplish/blue color remained with her skin. Each time she saw the color, she was reminded of the radiation treatments. It angered her that the treatments discolored her skin and left her tired and depressed. It angered her that the treatments attacked her feminine beauty -- attacked her . . . while foregoing healing her.

Five days ago Dr. Kirnan told her the tumor was the size of a pebble of sand. She stared at her left breast every morning since Dr. Kirnan told her radiation would not suffice for her. She stared at herself gape eyed, but only the image of one darkened nipple and one round, smooth breast came away from the mirror back to her. Staring at herself in the mirror reminded her of high school. While in high school, she stood in front of her mirror and tried to see cellulite on her thighs and the fattest parts of her buttocks. She never saw the cellulite. Still, she believed she was fat.

She twisted her mouth and gawked at her own reflection until her eyes ballooned. Raising her hand, she covered her left breast with her palm. Then she started to cry. She thought about her first training bra and how proud she'd been to snap it on. She thought about the last time she bought a bra -- size 38C. Shaking her head while she watched tears wet her face, she told herself that would change. Bowing her head, she freed the nightgown of her hand and stepped away from the mirror. She walked into the bathroom and took a shower.

When warm water ceased to sprout like spring rain in the shower, she took her body down, down into the tub, and, extending her legs until the soles of her feet went against the shiny, silver spigot, she stopped the tub drain. She leaned her head against the rim and soaked in a coconut oil bath. Cool air pricked her shoulder hairs. Fear scrambled her thoughts.

The bath-soak lasted twenty minutes. She pulled on a pair of jeans and a loose T-shirt and went into the kitchen. She ate a bowl of cottage cheese and drank a tall glass of purified water. She chuckled after she drank the water. She told herself she spent more money buying purified water than anybody she knew spent buying soda. Then she raised the half-full glass of water above her head and slammed it against the counter top. The glass broke apart. Its pieces sprinkled the counter top. Going to the center of the kitchen table for a roll of paper towels, she picked the broken glass up and tossed it inside the garbage can. When she went to the sink to wash her hands, the water stung her thumb. She stuck her thumb inside her mouth and sucked on it. After she pulled her thumb outside her mouth, she looked at it. Blood oozed out of her thumb. She watched the blood move down her hand. Then she started to cry again. "God," she wept aloud. "God, they're gonna cut me up. I'm gonna bleed and bleed and bleed until they're done. They're gonna cut me up and make me never be the same again."

The clock bonged. It was 10:00. A blue jay fluttered its wings against the kitchen window. She stared at the bird until it flew away from the window. Then she rounded the corner and entered her bedroom. The medical text. The one she bought from the bookstore two days ago. After she pulled it out of the bookcase lining her bedroom wall, she walked to her dresser and pulled out her stationery and a pen. Swallowing hard, she sat on the edge of her bed, and, using the medical text for support, she pressed down on the stationery with the pen.

*"Life for me has been good, very good. I am forever guarded with the sweetest memories. I didn't merely live then die. I lived and lived and lived and lived and lived. I'm going to go through with this second operation because of you, for you. I don't think it'll work – in the long run. For awhile I think I'll be okay, but not for a long time. I think you'll all out live me, but another day with you is worth being cut on again. I'm scared, but I'm ready. I love you all so very much, and I know that you truly love me. Because of your love, I will live forever – in your hearts. I'll follow you wherever you venture. I'll protect you with my unending love. I'll visit you when you're lonely. I'll give you the warmth of my love on nights that find you cold. You'll never be alone. You'll always be my closest friends. You gave me so much laughter. Goodness. Thanksgiving at grandma and grandpa's, then at our house. The little ones. They're all so big now. Coming out of high school and going into college. I can't believe how big Sophia is. Family reunions. Mama, remember how you told me Great-Grandma Armstrong started our family reunions? Started them when you were a little girl. Would tell who to cook what. Just thinking about it makes me want to laugh. Loud and hard. I can see her now. Barking out orders. You said she got it all done too. Everybody cooked and brought something. Even the men. Mama, you always told me Great-Grandma Armstrong wasn't for no store bought food. Had to be homemade. She wasn't having it any other way. I know that was some good grub. I'm glad we kept that tradition. Talk about some good cooking. I ate until my stomach was sore when we had our family reunions. And the games we played. Baseball. Horse shoes. Cards. Tug-of-war. Couldn't nobody tell me we didn't have fun coming up. I love you all so very much. You gave me so much hope. You're so much of the reason that I survived this long. Each time I think about you, I get warm all over. I am so very, very blessed to be a part of this family. God has been good-good to me. God even allowed me to experience the love of a good man before I departed this earth. How many years did I pretend that I didn't want to fall in love, didn't want a man to love me just for me? How long did I run from true love and affection and embrace abuse*

*and pain instead? But God knew. God heard my deepest unspoken prayers and sent me Dennis. I love you, Dennis. Outside my grandfathers, my father and my brothers, you are the most loving man I have ever met. You are like a dream. A man I dreamed up. It's as if you walked into my life straight out of my sweetest dream. You have been like an anchor in this troubled time in my life. You never ran. Not once did you cower. You never became angry with me for being sick. You never put me down or ridiculed me. Even after I had my lumpectomy, you always told me how beautiful I was and I could tell. I could tell, Honey. You meant every word of it. A woman knows when she's truly being loved. She knows. You are a true man, Dennis. The love of my life. My soul mate. I admire your strength, the way you go after your dreams. The way you refuse to quit, to ever give up. Hold to that spirit, that way of fight. It'll take you a long way up. I'll always love you, Dennis. I want you to continue to live after I'm gone. I want you to fall in love again. I want you to be happy, because I love you so very, very, very much."* She wiped away hurrying tears. *"From Portia to My Family and Dennis, the man I love."*

She folded the note and returned to her dresser. She dug through the small drawers at the top of her dresser until she found a tube of glue. Going back to her bed, she picked up the text and glued the folded note inside two pages in the middle of the text. Then she pulled books out of the bookcase and put them back in until the medical text was at the back of the case, behind a row of taller, thicker books.

Half an hour later, she telephoned Dennis, and, biting her bottom lip, she told him, "I'm ready." It wasn't long before Dennis pulled his Nissan Maxima inside Johnson Memorial Hospital's main parking lot.

Dennis stroked her hand while she looked at the clock on the wall. They'd been at the hospital for half an hour.

"Portia Fowler. Portia Fowler." The sound of her name echoing over the intercom sent her shoulders down. She knew her recovery bed was ready; she knew Dr. Kirnan was somewhere on the floor. Tugging on her skirt's hem, she turned sideways in her chair.

She picked her purple straw clutch purse out of the chair. She stood, pressed the purse against her left breast, and bowed her head.

Dennis took her hand inside his and gently squeezed it. "See you still have that straw purse."

She glanced at the purse. "It's from Aunt Lillian. If I didn't carry this purse nearly everywhere I went, she'd hunt me down."

He chuckled.

Plus she stole an old note from Mama that Great-Grandma Armstrong scribbled to Mama when she graduated from college with her teaching degree. I peeked at it. Most of the words are hard to make out. Great-Grandma Armstrong never did finish school. She couldn't read. Could barely write. A letter here. A letter there. You know. Aunt Lillian told me I couldn't read the note from top to bottom until after the operation." She laughed. "See how Aunt Lillian goes around fixing things?"

Wrapping his arm around her shoulder, he pulled her close and kissed the side of her face. "I love you."

As Dr. Kirnan promised, the surgery didn't take long. He sat with her before he worked to heal her body. While Dennis held her hand, she volleyed questions to Dr. Kirnan -- Will my chest hurt when I wake up? Will I bleed through my stitches? When can I go home? He told her -- You'll be groggy, scarcely in any pain, at the end of the surgery. You may bleed; that's why I took several pints of your blood prior to surgery. You should be resting at home in two to three days.

It was general anesthesia as Dr. Kirnan suggested and Portia nodded all the way into. It was no visitors except Dennis until she gained the nerve to look at her chest. She cried so hard in her recovery room following the surgery, Dennis climbed onto the edge of the bed and stretched out alongside her. He wrapped his arms around her waist and stroked the side of her face. "It's gonna be all right. God's with you. We're going to go through this together. We're going to grow through this together."

"I know." She wept softly. "You don't know how strongly I feel I need you."

"I'm not going anywhere." He kissed the side of her face. "You don't need me though. With God alone, you're all the woman you need to be and all you need."

She chuckled. "You're teaching the wrong course in college. You ought to be teaching men and women how to love each other."

He kissed the side of her face again. "You taught me all the good stuff I know. Before I met you I never did have a lot of good fortune when it came to women."

"I know you told me that before, but I still find it hard to believe."

"I never was a ladies man."

"Oh, now that I know. You are no skirt chaser. You don't have to tell me that. That's clear as day. I love you for that too. It makes it real easy for me to trust you."

"Know what made me this way? Faithful?"

"Watching your mom bring you up all by herself?"

"No."

"What then?"

He laughed. "All the cheating women I tried to love before I met you."

"What?"

"Yea. Instead of being a player I was the guy who all the women were playing."

"Now you know every last one of those women is on the phone with some friend crying about how there are no good men in the world."

They both laughed.

"And wishing they could find your phone number. You know how folks call up an old boyfriend or girlfriend as a last resource when the one they really wanted treats them badly?"

He chuckled.

"But they are not getting you. I'm never letting you go. Not while I'm on this side of the river." She shook her head. "Un-un. I'm not letting you go. Those fast, looking for Mr. Perfect women can just go cry in their tea."

They lay next to each other like that for hours until Portia drifted off to sleep. She was released from the hospital and resting at home before she stopped getting dressed in the dark.

"Baby, you can go in the bathroom. I'm finished in there."
She walked passed Dennis wearing her nightgown.

"Sure? You took a bath and are all washed up?" He watched her enter the bedroom. "I can wait if you're not finished."

Pulling her hair into a ponytail, she said, "No. I'm finished. Took my bath. Face is washed. Teeth brushed. The works."

He talked slowly. "Well. Okay. Then. I-I'm just going to go in her and take a quick shower. Call me if you need anything."

"I'm fine, Honey. Thanks." She waited.

The bathroom door closed and she lowered her shoulders. Taking in deep breaths, she walked toward her dresser. She'd taken a bath in the dark and poured water over the left side of her body instead of washing it with a rag. She stood in front of the dresser for a long time.

She turned and faced the doorway when she heard Dennis brushing his teeth in the bathroom. Not until now did it cross her mind that this was the first time they'd gone to church together.

A blue jay chirped and flew close to the window. She turned and watched the bird move through the sky. A moment later, the bird gone and the bedroom again quiet, she walked in front of her bedroom mirror and untied the top of her nightgown. She let the soft, pink fabric slide from her shoulders to the floor.

Her body uncovered, her mouth went open, but she was silent. She moved close to the mirror and rolled her gaze down to the place on her chest where her left breast used to be. As soon as she saw the flat, smooth surface on the left side of her chest, she raised her hand. She brushed her hand over her chest again and again. It startled her that there was no ugly hole.

"Here I am," she said to the mirror. "Here I am."

After he gargled and washed and dried his face, Dennis walked out of the bathroom. His eyes ballooned when he saw her without her nightgown on. His throat tightened the longer he looked at her. He swallowed hard. Walking toward her, he asked, "May I?"

She followed his gaze down to her chest. Then she nodded and whispered, "Yes."

He walked toward her slowly. Once at her side, he reached out his hand. "It's so smooth," he said. "Smooth as a baby's skin."

"I know," she told him. Then she placed her hand atop his and looked inside his eyes with intent. "Do you still feel like making love to me once I've recuperated from the surgery and am strong again?"

He smiled at her and said, "Only after you marry me first."

*Part 3*

*Wings*

## Chapter 10

### *Getting Wings*

It had been eight months since Portia's surgery. Dennis and she were married at Mount Zion Baptist Church on October 12, 1986. Flowers decorated the church aisles. At their reception, loosened champagne corks sailed toward the ceiling. "Bravo!" and "Cheers!" put noise in the air. Their love took them for walks through the park, laughing at the theatre, on dinner cruises and to bed for hours of warm, sensual love making.

The lovemaking was like wings. It touched every part of Portia's body. It put fire inside her eyes and moaning in her throat. It was a freeing episode that went on for her long after Dennis stopped touching her body. It went into her mind. It made her know her strength and her ability to love and to be loved came from her mother and her father. It made her know her deepest joys came from her great-grandparents, came from her grandparents, came from Ressey, Faye, Deborah, Craig, Edwin, Robert, Dennis and an Alabama heat that draped her shoulders with reddish brown clay colored skin

went down into a wishing well

full

full from its bottom all the way up to its brim.

To order additional copies of Portia
Call TOLL FREE: 1-800-929-7889 or
Mail $8.00 (shipping and handling is FREE) to:

Chistell Publishing
2500 Knights Road, Suite 19-01
Bensalem, PA  19020

## Visit us online at:
http://www.chistell.com